PANDORA'S BOX

Staying with her grandmother in Boston after her mother's death, Charlotte Haigh discovers the family cupboard conceals more skeletons than she bargained for. Charlotte is haunted by the unexplained death of her cousin Lois, and by a growing fear that someone in the family wants her out of the way. To complicate matters, Charlotte is attracted to Max Remmick, Lois' bereaved husband. Can she ignore his advice to leave the past alone? Or will she, in her search for the truth, uncover a story as shocking as it is tragic?

PANDORA'S BOX

PANDORA'S BOX

by

Marjorie Eccles

Magna Large Print Books
Long Preston, North Yorkshire,
England.

British Library Cataloguing in Publication Data.

Eccles, Marjorie
Pandora's box.

A catalogue record for this book is available from the British Library

ISBN 0-7505-1040-4

First published in Great Britain by Severn House Publishers, Ltd., 1995

Published in Large Print January, 1997 by arrangement with Severn House Publishers Ltd.

Magna Large Print is an imprint of
Library Magna Books Ltd.
Printed and bound in Great Britain by
T.J. International Ltd., Cornwall, PL28 8RW.

1

It was after eleven, the echoing late-night Boston streets were wet with rain, and I ran with the devil at my heels. A headlong escape from that rich, stifling house on Beacon Hill. Uncaring that no sensible young woman went alone at night, bait for muggers, kerb-crawlers, rapists. An easy target under the street lights in my white raincoat and red headscarf, the soft summer rain stinging my hot cheeks like midwinter sleet, blurring the lamps into golden dandelion clocks...lamps that were gaslit still, carefully preserving the past, like the tall elegant houses and the brick sidewalks, and the whole structure of my grandmother's society.

I ran on, down the hill, propelled by the need to get away from it all at any cost. My grandmother had just told me she was going to leave me her immense fortune, and I was angrier than I had ever been in my life.

A stitch in my side and the furious honking of a car—an automobile—wide as a London bus, telling me I had ignored a red 'Don't walk' sign, forced me to a stumbling half-run, half-walk. The common, the public gardens and down-town Boston left behind, I was at last in the waterfront area where Colin had his converted warehouse apartment. Colin, stocky, tough and dependable, my fellow Britisher. The only refuge I had, the only one without his own axe to grind. My footsteps rang in the dark echoing spaces, and as I searched the illuminated name plates outside the door, the beam of the lighthouse in the harbour swept the silent street.

I hadn't visited his apartment before, and Colin was plainly taken aback when he opened the door to see me there, panting and dishevelled.

'Charlotte! Well, well, well! Come away in.'

His soft Scottish voice welcomed, and his smile warmed me as he took my coat and ushered me into his living-room, his arm round my shoulders. Only then did it occur to me I might be intruding. Wagnerian music filled the lamplit room;

a whisky decanter, a glass and a book were on a low table by his chair. Everything spoke of a busy man relaxing after a hard day. Colin, like Max, his superior at the hospital, was a dedicated and obsessional worker, often staying on late, working into the small hours on a case. For a moment I felt guilty at invading this well-earned privacy, but he gave no sign of thinking any such thing. Indeed, he took one glance at my face as we came in from the lobby, and without saying anything else pulled a chair forward into the circle of lamplight, pressed me into it and poured me a generous whisky. I waved it away, shaking my head, but he would take no denial.

'Go on. There's some fresh coffee nearly ready in the kitchen, but drink this first. Doctor's orders.'

He curled my fingers round the glass and went through into the next room. Within minutes, he was back with the coffee tray, putting it on a low table before crossing to take the record off.

'Please don't—not on my account, Colin.'

'Too loud anyway,' he answered, taciturn and sparing of speech as always, and changed the disc for an old Joni Mitchell

I hadn't heard for years, the volume low. 'Drink up your dram,' he insisted quietly. Coming back to his chair opposite mine, he rested his elbows on his knees, rolling his own glass between his palms.

Obediently, I sipped my drink. I *had* needed it, more than I would have admitted; my teeth chattered against the rim of the heavy glass as I took a hasty gulp, but soon I began to feel calmer and leaned back in my chair. 'Colin—'

'No need to talk just yet, if you don't want. Give yourself a minute or two.'

He too leaned back, and I was grateful for the respite, for his unquestioning acceptance of my presence, because now I was beginning to realise just how difficult it was going to be to say what I had intended. In my usual reckless way, I had rushed out of the house without pause for thought...

The music slid softly, mournfully on, and the room I'd never seen before began to make its impression on me. He did himself well, Dr Colin Macintosh, I noticed with a jolt of surprise. The armchairs were grey suede, my feet sank into thick, noiseless tan carpets, one or two good modern reproductions faced me on the matt-finished off-white walls, and some small bronze sculptures stood here and there. There was an expensive hi-fi system and a well-stocked drinks table.

So what? Doctors were better paid over here than in Britain. And as one of the team of which Max was second-in-command, working on a rare form of cancer at one of the most famous hospitals in the world, he was bound to be receiving substantial monetary rewards as well as the more nebulous, if ultimately more worthwhile, ones of satisfaction and fulfilment. It wasn't however, the money which had evidently been expended on this flat which surprised me—rather that the liking for such luxury was the last thing I would have expected from this austere, red-haired Scottish Highlander.

Perhaps these things came to matter to a man living alone. Perhaps he felt the need for such comforts.

Almost simultaneous with the thought, the narrow bar of light shining beneath the door from the hallway into the low-lit room disappeared; then, soft as it was, I heard the click of the front door being closed. Colin must have seen and heard too, but he chose not to remark on it. So someone had been there when I arrived...someone he didn't want me to meet. A woman? Maybe. Colin was an attractive man, and his engagement to Harmony broken he wasn't the sort to hang around, mooning after her for ever.

I lifted my head and looked across at him. He was staring into space, almost as if he'd forgotten me, a man with something else on his mind, his chin square and stubborn. And it came to me then that even he might not be quite as detached from the subject of my grandmother's will as I had reckoned...supposing, for instance, that Harmony could be persuaded to change her mind.

They were going to hate me for it, all of them: Rowena and Sebastian, maybe Harmony, even Max. And I? Money of that quantity sprang from too much that I couldn't quite accept, too much that was tied up with power and privilege. Neither did I want the responsibility it entailed, nor the certainty that it would change my life, would inescapably tie me here, to America. But most of all, I disliked the thought that I was being manipulated, for some devious reason of her own, by Isabella. Was it because she knew it would put the cat right in amongst the pigeons that she had decided on this course of action, sent for me from England? From what I had already learned of my grandmother, I was willing to stake my fare home that this was so.

Six weeks ago I hadn't known of her existence, but when I first faced her, in that hot room with the fine white carved panelling, the washed silken Chinese carpets and the cut-glass bowls of hothouse orchids, I would have known her anywhere. For the black hair, still only threaded with silver though she must have been approaching eighty, the cameo profile, the pale matt skin, were the features I saw every day when I looked into my mirror. Even the eyes, hers unfaded still, having lost none of their sapphire-blue depth. I could only pray that time would not etch those harsh lines of pride, stubbornness and self-will on my face as it had on hers.

'So you are Lydia's daughter,' she stated, a small woman sitting facing me in an upright Colonial chair, her back straight as a ramrod. Standing, she was no taller than I was myself.

'Yes.'

'And you have only just discovered you

are my granddaughter—at twenty-seven?'

'As I wrote and told you, only when I found your letter amongst my mother's papers. After she died.'

Even now I found it difficult to think about the letter without shock. That my mother could have had this streak of vindictive cruelty in her was something I wouldn't believe. Not that! And yet...what had I really, deep down, known of her? Enough at least, I maintained, to know that she had never been one to bear a grudge, had indeed been almost too ready to excuse others and forgive. There had to be another explanation for the airmail letter I had found, unopened, "Return to Sender" written large and black across it, implacable. The name on the flap of the envelope was Mrs Ralph Stonor of Boston, Massachusetts, U.S.A. The firmness of my mother's handwriting across the envelope and the date of the postmark showed that it had been received long before her illness took hold, though not before she had been aware she was suffering from it.

The disease had been merciful only in that it was swift. Not too swift to prevent her making arrangements and preparations, however. In her quiet, persistent way she had demanded to be told the truth, faced it with courage, and, typically, her affairs had been left in immaculate order. I refused to believe she had simply forgotten the letter.

It lay there on top of the insurance policies, the deeds for the small stone house where we lived at the foot of the Pennines, and her modest will, leaving everything to me. The will of Lydia Haigh, née Stonor, American citizen, widow of Thomas Haigh, British schoolmaster.

No one died of a broken heart, they said, but I knew they did. I knew the rapid acceleration of my mother's illness was helped by the fact that she had refused to fight it when it made itself known only months after my father had collapsed with the massive coronary that had claimed his life.

'And you sit right there and tell me, Charlotte,' Isabella Stonor said in her clear, carrying voice, it's proper-Bostonian accent broadening the 'a' in my name, 'that not once did she ever speak of me?'

She had never spoken of any of her American relatives, nor of the place where she had been brought up. She might as well have arrived in England, new-minted at twenty-two, dropped from the skies.

'Why?' I had demanded of my father as I began to grow up and become curious about my origins. 'Why won't she talk about her family?'

'Charlotte, don't ask me. Your mother is essentially a very private person. There are things about her past life she doesn't like to talk about, things that upset her. And that I won't have.' Indeed he would not, he would never upset her himself, nor allow anyone else to do so. 'Maybe she'll tell you herself when you get older.'

Nothing would make him say any more, and she never had told me. I had to be content with half a background, Yorkshire grandparents who had both died early, and my only other relative my maiden aunt Elizabeth, Father's sister. But it was always there beneath the surface, that demanding urge to know: who was my mother? What had she left behind her in America? Why had she never gone back? And always present, too, that deep longing, whenever I, an only child, saw large families together, to be part of one.

'It's true,' I answered Isabella. 'I knew nothing of any of you.'

She stared at me without the slightest

trace of emotion on her face. Those eyes, so deep blue yet cold as marbles, met mine with an impenetrable look. And strangely, I felt utterly certain that she had found the hard facts as painful to accept as I did myself, that she still found them so, even though the situation had been going on for...how long? Before I was born? How many other letters had my mother returned, unopened? I felt an unexpected stab of pity for the old woman opposite. We were both caught up in the web of someone else's past, my grandmother and I. But Isabella had the advantage over me. She must have been aware of the reasons for it, the beginnings of it all.

'What made you write to me?' she asked at length, pouring us both a second cup of tea, brewed the English way, in a pot—not a teabag floating on the cup, its string dangling messily over the edge—and drunk out of delicate English Spode china.

'It was the least I could do, to let you know she had died. I found out about you when I opened your letter. I'm sure she meant me to open it, otherwise she wouldn't have left it there as she did. I couldn't understand why she had at first, then I began to think maybe she hadn't been able to forgive what had happened in the past—'

'She, forgive?' Isabella's voice cracked on harshness. '*She* was the one who ran away and never came back!'

'I'm sorry. Perhaps it was herself she couldn't forgive.'

'I'm such a coward, Charlotte, even now,' she had whispered, over and over again, as she bore her suffering with unbelievable courage.

I shut my mind to that remembered pain. 'Whatever it was, I think—I'm certain—it was her way of asking me to do what she couldn't bring herself to do.'

I heard a sharp intake of breath, and Isabella's eyes closed for a brief moment. Then she lifted her cup and took a sip of tea. She was ashy pale, but her hand was rock steady; the teaspoon in her saucer hadn't given so much as a tinkle against the china cup.

'It was her own choice. She ran away, she left all this...' Her thin white hands with their old woman's liver spots and her heavy rings made a gesture eloquent enough to include all the wealth and substance, the solidity and permanence of a powerful Stonor background. 'My daughter ran away and married a man who could give her nothing, nothing! She disgraced the Family.'

I sprang up, my anger scarcely controlled, my moment of pity for her vanished. 'If you've brought me over here to insult my father, then you've wasted your time and your airline ticket. He loved my mother deeply. They were happier together than any two people I've ever known.'

Happy indeed, self-sufficient, a magic, exclusive circle of two...

'Married to a schoolteacher?'

Her contempt dismissed as irrelevant the notion that happiness could or should enter into the business of marriage. For her, marriage was, incredibly, still a matter of finding a 'suitable' young man for one's daughter. That my father had been a good man, loved by everyone, counted as nothing. Or that he had been an excellent schoolmaster. He had loved teaching, leading young minds to stretch themselves in the right direction, and pupils he had taught thirty years before had come to his funeral, spoken of him with love. It had been his enthusiasm and dedication that had made me, too, take up teaching as a career. If I hadn't found it so wonderful, the fault lay in me, not my father.

'I think my coming here has been a mistake,' I said. 'There doesn't seem to be anything we can say to each other.'

Why indeed had she sent for me to come at all? She seemed bent only on widening the gulf of misunderstanding between us.

'Sit down, Charlotte.'

Automatically, I obeyed the cool, clear command that brooked no disobedience. 'I want no talk of going home, yet. I want you to promise me you will stay—a little while longer, at any rate.'

'No, I can't promise that.'

I met her challenge with equal stubbornness. Antagonism flashed across the space between us, and Isabella gripped the arms of her chair until her knuckles showed white and sharp. 'You are Lydia's daughter, sure enough! Just like her, selfish and wilful! Perhaps it would be better if you did go home.'

I took a deep breath, holding on to my temper, 'I think it would. Other considerations apart, I have a job to go back to.'

I had been lucky that my position in the history department of Ellerman Hall

Comprehensive had been held open for me while I nursed my mother. A supply teacher had been brought in to stay until the end of term, for which I had to thank Graham Taylor, my department head. Poor old Graham...I liked him, and would always be grateful to him, but his anxious, devoted brown eyes and his eager-to-please manner reminded me too much of our old spaniel to inspire the faintest excitement in me. So because I couldn't encourage his hopes that one day I would allow our friendship to become more than that, I mustn't accept anything more from him. 'I have to be back in England when term starts,' I said with as much firmness as I could manage.

'Ah yes, your—career.' Isabella's eyebrows lifted. Her dry inflection gave my career as much importance as selling raffle tickets.

It was partly the recollection that she'd gone to some trouble to find out her daughter's whereabouts in England, partly the memory of that letter she'd written—on the surface a flat, formal request for my mother's signature on a document relating to some family property, but in which I had fancied I had caught the merest hint of remorse, even pleading—that stopped me walking out there and then. Instead, I stayed. I would not make promises I had no intention of keeping, but neither would I run away. I had just found out something surprising about myself. It wasn't only my grandmother's looks I had inherited. Just as much as the autocratic old woman before me, I too had the capacity to fight.

'All right then. For a week or two, I'll stay. But one thing I must know. Why did my mother leave home?'

Isabella's lips, however, remained firmly shut. She either would not, or could not, tell me.

'Come back, Charlotte.'

The record had ended without my noticing, and Colin was eyeing me expectantly. He must be burned up with curiosity, wondering why I'd come running to him at nearly midnight, obviously in some distress. And he'd every right to feel entitled to an explanation, which I knew now I couldn't give. He poured coffee, handed me a cup.

'Something happened tonight. It upset me rather. I wanted to ask your advice...'

‘But?’

‘But now I’ve had time to think it over.’ I despised myself now for giving in to the impulse to run and place the burden on someone else’s shoulders, even shoulders as broad as Colin’s. Besides, caution, usually foreign to my nature, had stepped in, warning me that this latest thing, which had passed between myself and my grandmother not an hour ago, had better stay between the two of us, since I wasn’t going to accept her money, not on any terms, much less the conditions she imposed. ‘Colin, I’m sorry, but it’s best after all if I didn’t talk about it, not yet.’

‘Up to you, of course.’ He shrugged, giving me one of his deep, penetrating Highland looks. ‘Though it’s never a good idea to keep a thing bottled up, wouldn’t you say?’

‘It’s not a question of that. Look, I know I’m being maddening, but it really would be better to let it ride at present. I know I should have thought of that before I came bothering you, only I was a bit rattled...’

He raised a wry ginger eyebrow at such obvious understatement. ‘Mad at you? Don’t be daft, girl!’

The telephone rang, stridently, making

us both jump. Quickly, Colin crossed the room. 'Hello? Oh, Max.' His voice took on a guarded coolness; he became at once more formal, work-orientated. I always had the impression, without any foundation on which to base my assumptions, that they didn't like each other. Colin, nothing if not ambitious, would never do anything to prejudice his chances in that direction, however, and he was always extra polite to Max. 'Charlotte?' he repeated. 'Yes, she's here—what?' He listened for several minutes, whilst I absently fiddled with the bits and pieces on the table near me, my ears pricked at the mention of my name. 'I see. No, no, of course she isn't...'

I found my fist clenched round what I held, something which dug sharply into my palm. When I opened my hand, I was looking at one of a pair of earrings of some violet-coloured polished stone set in filigree silver, which had been placed on the table as if the wearer had found them uncomfortable, slipped them off and forgotten them...

'...okay then. Bye now.' Putting the receiver down and turning to me, Colin said, 'Max is coming to fetch you in a few minutes.'

'What?'

'There's an emergency back at the hospital—a patient who needs special monitoring. Max has been there all evening. The chief's taken over now, but he needs me there as well. Max'll be picking you up on his way home.'

There wasn't anything I could say to this, no objection I could put forward in the circumstances. But being dragged back to the house on Beacon Hill like a naughty schoolgirl by Max Remmick was something I would have done practically anything to avoid.

2

The rain had stopped, and a stiff breeze was blowing draughtily around the apartment block as Max and I stepped outside. The waterfront lights shone on still-wet cobbles, were reflected in the sea. Behind us the city was a lighted backdrop against the dark sky. Ahead, an aircraft came in low over Logan airport across the harbour, its landing lights winking; another lifted off diagonally on backswept wings and roared off into the clouds.

Max, courteous and remote, held open the passenger door of his car for me, a '79 Pontiac, navy-blue, sleek and gleaming, then walked round to the other side and slid in beside me. He seemed even more than usually preoccupied, and since I was still smarting from the arbitrary way I'd been dealt with we spoke little as he drove through the city, past the Faneuil Hall and the Old State House, the spectacularly tall lighted columns of high-rise blocks gleaming on other homelier buildings with historic associations. The moon came out and a shaft of brilliant white light silvered the great gilded dome of the "New" State House as he skirted the common, outlining his unsmiling profile. I couldn't see his eyes, but I knew they'd be remote, gleaming with something like scorn as they too often seemed to do when they rested on me.

Lamps glowed through the window of the round bay of the tall, narrow brick house with steps leading directly off the street, its area bordered with wrought-iron railings that matched the ironwork of the second floor balcony. A gas lamp cast its reflection on to immaculate black paintwork, the great handsome polished brass doorknocker and the scrubbed stone steps. Virginia creeper softened the brick, and the trees lining the sidewalk threw tremulous patterns against the walls. An ocean separated us from England, but here in this part of the city, amongst these wealthy homes with their quotations from English architecture, we might, as Isabella was fond of repeating, have been in a London square.

Max parked the car economically beside the kerb and followed me as I mounted the steps. Before he could put his key in the door it was opened from inside by Isabella's housekeeper, already wearing her old-fashioned blue woollen dressing-gown, her grey hair pinned up for the night.

'Mary. You haven't waited up, I hope? Nothing wrong?'

'No, no, Dr Remmick, I was on my way to bed.'

'Mrs Stonor's asleep now?'

'She is, thank God.'

He looked relieved, clasped her shoulder momentarily. I felt a small tug of alarm at the words, in the unspoken communication they exchanged, but then Mary McDermott nodded reassuringly, a nod that included me, and smiled. Native-born Irish, she had never completely lost the lilt of her brogue, nor the twinkle in her eyes. 'I've left sandwiches and coffee, but don't go staying up all night now,' she admonished as she bade us goodnight and mounted the stairs, her pace brisk, her figure trim for all her sixty-odd years.

I made to follow her, pausing with my hand on the newel post. 'Goodnight, Max. Thanks for bringing me home.' Try as I might, I couldn't make my thanks more cordial.

'Come in here a minute, will you? Something I want to say to you.'

I hesitated. He could be pleasant enough when he wanted, but in this mood he was forbidding. Then I followed him into the long, beautiful room that stretched the length of the house, its old white panelling a foil for rose-shaded lamps, blue and gold Chinese carpets, curtains of ruby velvet. On a table stood a Thermos jug and a covered plate of sandwiches which he inspected and pronounced to be chicken. I shook my head at the offer of one, but accepted the cup of coffee he handed me. I looked at the cups on the tray. There were two. 'My grandmother rang you at the hospital?'

'No, Mary did.'

'Mary?'

'She was worried, the way you rushed out without saying where you were going. However, I figured where you'd be.'

I flushed at both implication and criticism, especially since I knew the latter to be justified. It had been thoughtless to have left like that, without telling anyone where I was going. My only excuse was the shock which had wiped other considerations clean from my mind.

And so Mary had rung Max. Naturally. Max, who could always be relied on to sort things out, who was accustomed to making decisions and coping with emergencies every day as a matter of course. Even sitting at ease, long legs stretched out, his collar and tie were immaculate and his straight fair hair was totally unruffled; he looked authoritative, dependable, instinctively in command.

Yet to me Max Remmick was an enigma. I couldn't make him out, why he chose to live here. How could he bear to be surrounded by so many memories of Lois, his dead wife...my cousin whom I'd never known, Isabella's adored granddaughter? She had been dead for twelve months now and I would have thought that Max, still only in his mid-thirties, self-contained and fulfilled in an absorbing and successful career, would have cut loose from the unhealthy reminders of past sorrows that filled every corner of this house, where remembering Lois was an obsession, almost a cult. Yet here he stayed, where it was impossible to get away from her. Had he loved her so very much?

My grandmother wouldn't let Lois die. She kept her alive, everywhere. In this room, in the dining-room, on staircases and landings, in studio photographs, framed snapshots, the portrait in oils over the mantel, adverts cut from glossy magazines during her brief period as a model...brief, because it was unthinkable that any Stonor woman should be serious about a career. And on the table in front of Isabella's bedroom window, like a shrine, flanked by silver candlesticks, stood a little silver-gilt figurine of her in what I imagined was typical pose. Head thrown back, chin confidently lifted. Enviable figure and long legs shown to advantage by the swimsuit she wore. Holding two dogs straining at the leash.

Oh yes, Lois had been beautiful. And the family genes that had dictated my likeness to Isabella had worked here, too. Lois was the very spit of my mother, chestnut-haired, hazel-eyed...but cat's eyes, Lois's were, that followed you around, watchful and secretive, the eyelids slightly lowered.

I said to Max, 'I'm sorry if I upset my grandmother. I suppose Mary told you we quarrelled.'

'I don't imagine it was all your fault.' His voice held a note of dry amusement. He had a short, assured way of speaking, slightly pedantic in expression sometimes; cultured New England, not noticeably American. 'Isabella can be pretty trying at times.'

'Trying! She was...impossible.'

'Let me guess what it was all about. One—she told you she intended making you her heiress...correct?'

'Yes,' I said shortly, taken aback. 'She did.'

'And two—you made a pretence of not wanting it.'

I thought at first I must have misheard him. 'A pretence?'

'My dear Charlotte,' he said, in a way that indicated I was very evidently not his dear Charlotte. 'I'm only stating the obvious. You must have realised the possibilities when you found out who your grandmother was—to put it at its crudest.'

This was American outspokenness, I reminded myself, not deliberate provocation. 'It was she who sent for me to come here, you know that,' I said steadily. 'And she has two other granddaughters, remember? Not strangers to her, either, as I was.'

'Which could be to your advantage. Now

now, don't take offence. She's very fond of Harmony, but she isn't a woman to let that make any difference.' He broke off to eat some of his sandwich. 'And as for Rowena—you've seen how the land lies there.'

Isabella had had two other children besides my mother: her eldest daughter Ellen, who had been Rowena's mother... and Richard, the heir, who had crashed his private plane, killing himself and his socialite wife and leaving two daughters, Lois and her much younger sister Harmony. This was family history. So now that Lois was dead, too, there remained only my cousins Harmony and Rowena. And myself.

I didn't understand what Max's references to either of them had meant. 'Why is my grandmother so against Rowena? And her husband?'

'Why?' He laughed shortly, and without really answering, he said: 'Do you see Isabella leaving the Stonor fortune where Sebastian Garth can get his hands on it? No, of course you can't. I don't believe, either, that it can have escaped your notice that you're therefore not badly positioned to come in for the lot.'

'I don't think I like your implications. But in any case, it's academic. I don't believe she intends me having anything at all, despite what she's said.' Surprising myself, I found I believed what my subconscious must have been working on. 'She'd like everyone to think so, I daresay, but that's as far as it will go. She knows I'd never skip to her tune, for one thing...though she won't stop at using me,' I finished bitterly, realising the astuteness with which she'd already manoeuvred me for her own ends, anticipating I would do just what she intended—broadcast her plans, and so stir up the mud. That I hadn't done so had been more due to Colin's insistence that I took my time before blurting out the whole thing than any misjudgement of my character on Isabella's part.

'Indeed she won't. There's very little Isabella would stop at for the continuation of the family.' The briefest of meaning pauses. 'But don't make the mistake of underestimating her. If she has said it, she means it, take it from me...though you may be halfway right. She respects anyone who stands up to her. And,' he added softly, 'I must insist—pardon me for speaking so plainly—I must insist you're smart enough to realise the mileage there is in that for you.'

It was there, on the tip of my tongue, the last thing I ought to have said, but he had hurt me, too. 'And not only for me. You're a hot favourite as well, aren't you? She told me she always intended leaving everything to Lois—so why not you, in her stead? I suppose that's why you stay here, dancing attendance on her?'

There was a deadly little silence. My temper had led me too far, something it was too often inclined to do, something of which I wasn't proud. 'I'm sorry, I shouldn't have said that.'

'Maybe not,' he replied, reasonable, cool, distanced. 'But I can take as well as give. Especially since it's so far off the truth.'

'Look,' I said, wanting to explain myself. 'I don't know what impression I've given, but I'm not the money-grabbing sort. I wouldn't know what to do with it—most people wouldn't. Would *you* know what to do with millions of dollars?'

'I might just be able to put up with the inconvenience.'

I drew in a deep breath.

He weighed me up with a small, cynical

smile, then he inclined his head. 'Since I'm hardly likely to benefit from such, I'll tell you yes, I would. I know just what I'd do with it. I'd start up a clinic for research and treatment. I'd pay the best people I could find to work there, see they never went short of a penny for equipment. I'd never again see a life lost simply through lack of funds. Maybe some patients might have their life expectancy extended. They might just, some day, be cured.'

I think he meant simply to snub me, to shut me up. I don't for a moment think he was aware how lit from within, how dynamically alive he sounded, until he saw the effect of what he'd said on me. I was like a pricked balloon. There was no room for anger in me after that. Not anger, but a small cold voice whispering that such idealism could be more dangerous than greed.

'You did ask,' he said, laconic once more.

'Then can't you understand me at all? You have your own values, why shouldn't I have mine?'

'How should I know? I don't know anything about you, do I, Charlotte-from-England?' But for the first time since I'd met him, I felt him beginning to look at me and consider me seriously. He leaned slightly towards me, so that I saw the dark circles of exhaustion beneath his eyes, the stray threads of silver in his hair. Unexpectedly, amusement tugged at the corners of his mouth. 'I don't even know if you always look so glum, or whether you smile occasionally.'

'Smile?'

'That facial expression signifying pleasure! I haven't seen you smile once—really smile, let alone laugh—since you came here.'

It must have been the first time, ever, that anyone had said *that* to me. I laughed as easily as I cried or lost my temper, and I hoped a deal more often than either. 'There hasn't been much to smile at recently, especially since I've been in Boston,' I said, stung into self-pity.

'Then why stay? Why not get the hell out of it and go home?'

The ball was neatly fielded. Yet he must have suspected the ambivalence in me, the wish to do just as he suggested and leave my grandmother and her devious plotting three thousand miles behind—a wish conflicting with the obstinate determination to see my mother vindicated—because he said, more gently. 'I'll just say this, though...if you do leave, don't do it in anger. Even an old warrior like Isabella Stonor is vulnerable. Hit her where it hurts and she'll crumple like the rest of us.'

Isabella? She had so much strength, it was impossible to think of her in that light. And did age automatically give anyone the right to ride roughshod over the feelings and emotions of others?

He stood up suddenly, looking down at me. 'One thing more, then I'll let you get to bed. If you do stay here, with all that implies, don't be surprised to find you have enemies. People will go a long way to get their hands on the sort of money your grandmother has, and'—the return to his original theme had already perceptibly hardened his attitude against me once more—'don't expect any help from me.'

The warning chilled me to the bone.

He leaned forward, took my hands and pulled me to my feet. 'Come on, it's been a long day, and you look as if you could use some sleep.'

He had large hands, good, doctor's hands, firm and well-shaped. I could feel their warmth flowing into mine, warming my cold fingers, and suddenly I wished, as fervently as I had wished for anything in my life, that this man could be my friend rather than my enemy.

Isabella never came downstairs until lunch time, but no matter how early I went in to see her, as I had formed the habit of doing directly after breakfast, she was invariably up and dressed, her hair neatly arranged in its habitual severe twist, sitting at her hickory wood desk, dealing with her correspondence.

There was usually a large amount of mail, domestic bills and charge accounts with the "best" shops in Boston to be settled, arrangements for donations to various charities, on many of which she was still a committee member. Before I came, she had answered all her letters by hand; when she found I could type, albeit with only two fingers, my services had been instantly commandeered. I didn't object, hoping that while we were so occupied we wouldn't be drawn into controversy.

I was also helping her with something else. She had restarted a task begun by her late husband, my grandfather Ralph Stonor, gathering together the family papers with the eventual hope that they could some day be written up and maybe published. Lois had agreed to help her with this—been press-ganged might, I suspected, have been a better way of putting it—and I was "allowed" to continue where she had left off, sorting through the bills, diaries, letters and other documents accumulated over the years by Stonors who never threw anything away.

Despite the creepy feeling that was increasingly overtaking me, a feeling of being in more ways than one forced into a dead woman's shoes, I was swiftly becoming hooked as I came across fascinating insights into the lives of these long-dead, pioneering Stonors, hardworking yeomen farmers of unshakable religious conviction who had sailed from England in the seventeenth century to find freedom of conscience in the New World, become whalers in Nantucket, shipowners and bankers in Boston. These were my family, too. There had even been a Charlotte Stonor, two generations ago, perhaps the one my mother had named me for...I was profoundly glad Lydia's tastes hadn't inclined her to perpetuate the name of Thankful, or even Patience or Prudence, wildly inappropriate as they would have been for me.

Isabella wore a secret smile as she noted my involvement. When two people work together at some task there is a link forged, however tenuous, and I knew that enlisting my help was only part of her real purpose, to tie another of those knots in the net she was hoping to weave around me, so that when the time came she could draw it tighter...but I felt in no danger, as long as I was aware of what she was doing.

I was finishing my breakfast in the dining-room at the front of the house before going up to her, when Mary McDermott popped her head round the door and told me Harmony was telephoning, asking for me.

'Hi, Charlotte!' Harmony said as I picked up the receiver. 'Listen, I'm in a payphone and I've just put my last dime in, so—quick...how about meeting me and doing something together today?' Her voice broke into laughter. 'Hit the Freedom Trail together, maybe? I've promised to do that so often with you, listen, I feel really guilty, you know?'

The warmth of that famed American hospitality flowed down the line, with the lilt of her voice, vibrant and full of life, as if she found the world and everything in it wonderful. 'That's nice of you,' I said, 'but it'll wait, or I can go myself. I know you're snowed under with work.'

'Oh, it's still way off to semester finals—well, three days—and anyway, I already studied two hours today.'

I could see her in my mind's eye, with her pretty pale-gold hair disguised by the Afro-tangle in which she was currently wearing it, her piquant, friendly face, the small, gold-rimmed spectacles like an old Swiss clockmaker's, and her wide, white American smile. And I remembered Max's opinion of me last night. Dreary old me, who never smiled. 'I'd love to come,' I told her. 'Where shall we meet?'

'Great! How about Harvard Yard at say, about—er—eleven? By the Memorial Church. I'll be wait—'

Before she could finish, the line cut off.

Back in the dining-room, Mary was beginning to clear the table. I swallowed the rest of my coffee and put my used crockery together, wondering about getting over to Harvard in Cambridge. Why had Harmony suggested going over there? It would have been more logical to have started in Boston, this side of the river, if we were going to follow what was known as the Freedom Trail. They were great on history, the Bostonians, proud of being the first colonists to strike a blow for freedom and independence from England two hundred years ago, and this tour of the historical monuments had been worked out to show the story as and where it happened, here in Boston.

I could of course take the small car my grandmother had ordered to be put at my disposal for the duration of my stay, but, well... To begin with, I wasn't mad on the idea of driving it through what I had seen of Boston's traffic—freeways, thruways or what-have-you notwithstanding. Secondly, I had so far firmly resisted this particular bribe of Isabella's...and after what had happened last night, my determination was strengthened. Simple enough anyway to go by underground, the subway.

A car drew up outside. Mary looked out of the window and made a cluck of disapproval which she tried unsuccessfully to turn into a cough. 'Your cousin Rowena,' she announced. '*And* her husband. I'll let them in.'

'I'll go, Mary.'

She was plainly relieved to be allowed to get on with clearing the room herself, being one of those women who didn't really like anyone else interfering in her duties, which were carefully timetabled and laid out by herself, geared to running the house perfectly, with the help of what she called "scrubwomen".

'Hello, there,' Rowena said in her quick, brittle way, and Sebastian, entering behind her, greeted me with a drawling 'Good morning, cousin Charlotte,' and a kiss I wasn't quick enough to dodge completely. It landed on my ear, and I resisted the impulse to take my handkerchief out and scrub the spot.

They followed me into the long drawing-room, where Sebastian immediately folded his long frame into a chair and lit a cigarette, although he knew Isabella detested smoking in the house. 'I have no wish to hurry you, Ro my love, but I have to be with some people downtown by ten,' he said.

'Aren't you coming up with me to see Grandmother?'

'Do I ever, if I can help it?'

Rowena looked at him edgily, clearly

torn between coercing him into going up with her and provoking an almost certain exchange of words between him and Isabella, and leaving him downstairs, in which case Isabella would be sure to remark on his discourtesy in not going up to see her.

Rowena was as elegantly got up this morning as always, dressed for business, this time in a white linen suit with a brown silk rose on the lapel, which suited her chestnut Stonor colouring, her wide hazel eyes. She might have been as good-looking as Lois if she hadn't been so tense and nervy, which had the effect of dragging her face into taut, strained lines and making her slimness almost shadow-thin. She stood restlessly twisting the clasp of the soft chocolate-brown suede bag which hung from her shoulder, a muscle twitching in her cheek. Finally, she said, 'All right, but if she asks for you, you're to come up immediately she rings.'

'Sure, but don't you be long.'

The sound of her high heels tapping on the parquet receded, and Sebastian gave a slight groan, putting his hand theatrically to his eyes. 'I believe I could use some coffee, cousin Charlotte. I—er—don't suppose there's anything stronger around here?'

'At this time in the morning? Coffee or nothing.' I had soon learned that finesse was wasted on Sebastian Garth, and went into the kitchen where Mary was already heating up what was left of the breakfast coffee.

'Didn't I know it's always the first thing he asks for? Sure he was born with a hangover, that one.' She winked and poured the now bitter-looking brew into a cup. 'This should fix him.'

We exchanged a grin and I carried the coffee back to Sebastian. We made desultory conversation while he drank it and waited for Rowena, though we had no common meeting-ground and I never knew how to answer the patronising remarks which seemed to be his way of talking with women. In appearance he was light-haired, tall, with a small moustache, and he looked at life from under half-closed lids, cynically amused, never going out of his way to antagonise anyone, but seeming to manage it all the same. Yet he was nobody's fool. I had caught more than once the flash of a sharper intellect than he chose to project.

I asked him how business was. 'Not

good. Money's tight and people are hanging on to their antique silver and gold, and nobody seems keen on buying jewellery, either.' He smiled, world-weary, and conversation lapsed again. This morning he was evidently finding my company even less stimulating than usual. He fidgeted with the morning papers, yawned, looked several times at his watch and occasionally with a hooded glance at me. Finally he said, 'I'm beginning to wonder if there isn't more than a streak of the martyr in my dear wife. Why else do you think she insists on coming over here so often to see Isabella—when all it does is to reduce her to a pulp?'

There was no answer to a statement of such undoubted truth. Rowena was a difficult woman. For all her spiky sophistication, she had a certain naïvete about her. Frequently, she seemed to be unsure and hesitant, especially when confronted with Isabella. And yet she went out of her way to please the old woman, getting nothing for it but freezing contempt. I made some noncommittal remark to Sebastian, but he hardly seemed interested in my reply, getting up as I spoke and going to stand in front of the oil-painting of Lois that hung over the marble mantel. 'It isn't as if she could expect—' he began, breaking off to give me another of those veiled glances. 'You know why your grandmother hates the sight of her of course? Because she isn't Lois. Because she's alive, and Lois isn't. Because nobody in the whole goddam world will ever make up for that! So remember it, cousin Charlotte, is my advice to you. However much we all try to keep in with old Isabella—'

Did I imagine the undertone of hostility, even threat, beneath that slightly derisive manner? I couldn't be sure, especially as he stopped talking when Rowena's returning footsteps were heard in the hall.

She was frowning when she came in and her face was flushed. 'Now what's wrong, dear?' Sebastian asked, with patient exasperation.

'She's insisting on going to the Point next week...after everything that happened there.' Rowena, who never let anger get the better of her, stopped and bit her lip, then turned to me. 'She says she wants to show you the place. I hope you haven't been encouraging her?'

'I've never heard of—where did you say?

Nor her plans to go there. Why? Should she have mentioned them to me?'

Arched eyebrows raised, she looked at me without answering. Sebastian drawled, 'It's something of a miracle she hasn't, then. She lives for the summer months she spends there—Stonor's Point is the family property up on the coast. And once a year all the rest of us are bidden there too, on Grandfather Stonor's birthday as ever was. He's been in his grave above a quarter of a century, but still we go there to celebrate it, one big, happy family party!'

'She can't,' Rowena said tensely. 'She can't be serious. It'll bring it all back again. And you know what she is when she's upset.' Once more she stopped herself, exchanging wary looks with Sebastian.

'Bring what back?' I asked, since neither appeared to be going to volunteer the information.

At first I thought I wasn't going to get an answer, then Rowena turned to me again, and all her restless movements were stilled into one tense, motionless moment. 'Didn't you know?' she asked. 'Lois was drowned there, last year.'

3

There was all the promise of a fine day, yet a bright fire burned in the hearth, and Isabella's room was stifling. She never seemed to feel the heat; I knew if I touched her fingers they would be like ice. The fragrance of the scented orchid she loved, from the orchid house at her country home—this, I saw now, must be Stonor's Point—added its own sickly claustrophobia to the air. She had lifted one lurid magenta bloom, splotched with poison green, from a small arrangement in front of the silver-gilt statuette of Lois, and was examining the rest critically when I came in.

'Have they gone?' She turned from the window, her mouth a tight line of disapproval.

'A few minutes ago. Sebastian had an appointment, and Rowena had to be at the restaurant.'

Isabella crumpled the dying orchid tightly in her hand and threw it on the fire, where it spat for a moment before it flamed and died. *'Rowen's Place!* How impossibly vulgar—what would her grandfather have said to her wasting the money he left her? Between that and Sebastian Garth there soon won't be a cent left. I'm only surprised he allowed her to put money into it anyway—so much less for him to squander. Oh, she's such a fool?'

I found Isabella's attitude not only unjust but curiously out of date, and unconvincing too. Old as she was, she wasn't out of touch with the contemporary world, and since the fortunes of the family of which she was so proud had unarguably been based on trade, there scarcely seemed to be any foundation for her opposition to Rowena's business venture, a restaurant overlooking the harbour, which she had bought and now managed.

Isabella crossed to the desk and sat on her chair, an upright little figure in her smoke-blue silk dress, its softly-rolled collar revealing the firmness of a throat and chin-line a woman forty years her junior might have envied. Her heavy, sparkling rings emphasised the thinness of her fingers as she drummed them on the desk. 'She's trying to stop me going to Stonor's Point next week.'

'Do you think it's wise to go?'

'Ah—so they *have* been talking to you!'

I judged that an unprofitable deviation to follow. 'Wise in terms of the journey was what I meant. How far is it?'

'Not too far out of Boston by car, even for an old woman. It's quite ridiculous. Never yet have I missed summering there since I was married, and this time I've planned for you to see it, too.'

'No.'

'No, Charlotte? Why ever not?' She chose to show amazement. All the family went, at least for the special party always held on her husband's birthday. Guests were invited as well as the family; it was an annual event now expected of her. 'I think you must change your mind...I've planned for you to be there,' she repeated, as if that clinched it. 'It's a lovely house, you'll adore it. Your grandfather's grandfather built it for his bride.'

Rapid calculation told me this must have been Ezekiel Stonor, that Boston shipowner who had compounded the family fortunes by cannily marrying an heiress, he who took cold baths morning and evening and ate but one frugal meal a day. Isabella hadn't one drop of his blood in her veins, but without doubt she was a spiritual descendant, one of the same unswerving will, the same iron determination.

'I see no valid reason why I shouldn't go there this year as usual,' she was continuing. 'Nor indeed does Max. They need have no fear. Lois's death wasn't the first tragedy I've survived. Stonor's Point holds no terrors for me.' Her eyes strayed to the little figurine poised under the window, and for a passing moment the pinched look about her mouth gave the lie to her denial. 'I *will* go—and I shall come back. My husband was born in this house, and I shall die in it.'

Her reasoning was understandable if one realised that, by marrying into the Stonor family, she considered herself just as much one of them as if she had been born to the name. Just as she wished me to become one, a Stonor not only through my mother, but by taking their name as well. I watched her as she fell silent, staring at the polished surface of the desk, absorbed in private thoughts and old griefs. *Not the only tragedy*, she had said. What else had happened at Stonor's Point? If I probed gently, now, would I find out? I looked again at that rigidly-held pose, at that closed, hidden face, and I knew I wasn't near enough to her, if I or anyone ever could be, to attempt to try.

Something stirred in my subconscious, and slowly surfaced. Something she had said to me the day before when I'd been working on the family papers. I had discovered they only went up to about 1940, but there were more, she had said, in Grandfather Stonor's study at their summer home, more recent ones. And that might mean...some clue to my mother's past.

I was suddenly on fire to go there. I was also, however, learning enough not to betray my thoughts to Isabella, and still wary of committing myself, afraid of being drawn willy-nilly into her intrigues. I said, 'Could we begin your letters? I've arranged to meet Harmony at eleven. She's going to show me some of Boston's history.'

'Oh?' In an instant, she had put aside her preoccupation, and the blue eyes were snapping with that sharp awareness. 'Can she spare the time?' *And should you be encouraging her to do so?* was the unspoken comment that accompanied the look.

Annoyed that I found excuses necessary, for myself as well as for Harmony, I said, 'She's really been working very hard. She'll get through, I'm sure.'

Where her youngest granddaughter was concerned, all Isabella's objections to women having a career seemed miraculously to have disappeared. Since marriage to Colin now seemed out of the question, she pushed Harmony relentlessly towards getting her degree, quizzing her unremittingly about her progress every time she came to the house. Harmony submitted amiably enough, but had wary, astute old Isabella nevertheless sensed the rebellion in her, what she was talking of doing?

'Leave the letters today.' Abruptly, she pushed them aside. 'Go and meet her. That foolish child, throwing away her chances like that!' Startled, I looked quickly at her, before realising it was Harmony's broken engagement she was talking about, and it crossed my mind, not for the first time, how odd it was that Isabella should so favour a match with Colin Macintosh. True, he was well launched into a promising career, and there was no denying, if that was the way you thought, that he would make anyone an enviable husband—anyone except a Stonor.

A prince didn't look at a pauper. A Stonor, one of the social elite, could look higher than that.

'Go and enjoy your history. Before you leave, let Mary know you won't be in for lunch, if you please. And Charlotte, you may remind Harmony we shall all be going to the Point as usual this year. I shall make arrangements today.' Her hand was already on the telephone.

I caught back a retort at that gently-stressed "all". No harm could come of letting her think she had dragooned me into going there with her when now, suddenly, nothing would have kept me away.

I turned to go and some thought, I don't know what, perhaps pity for her, caught up in the prison of her own outmoded opinions and prejudices, regret that I couldn't make myself be as she wanted me, made me pause beside her chair. On an impulse, astonishing myself, I dropped a kiss on her dry old cheek.

And Isabella smiled. There was triumph in it, yes, but also a certain affection, and in its dazzling reflection I caught a glimpse of the girl she had been, who had once, for charity, had young men queueing up to buy her kisses for a dollar apiece.

Picking up Sebastian's empty coffee cup on the way and going into the kitchen, I found Mary McDermott ironing the last of the pile of table linen that had been stiffly starched in the old-fashioned way. Clouds of steam rose up, and as she rubbed the iron back and forth, smoothing the linen to a crisp gloss, a warm, soapy smell permeated the kitchen. I took the cup to the sink, washed it and left it to drain.

'Do you good to get out, you look a mite peaked,' Mary remarked after I had told her about lunch. 'Not still fretting over that bother last night, are you? You shouldn't take things to heart so. Your mother, God rest her, was always the same, and much good it did her.'

'My mother?'

In two strides I was standing in front of her, gripping the edge of the ironing board. 'You were here when my mother was? You *knew* her?'

Her busy hands came to rest, and she put the iron on its asbestos stand, looking at me with blank astonishment. 'To be sure I knew her. I've been with Mrs Stonor nearly forty years.'

'Oh—I didn't know!' A leap of gladness filled me. 'Tell me about her, Mary. What was she like when she was young?'

'Like?' A smile lifted the corners of her mouth. 'She was lovely. Lovely like Lois, yes, but—lovely inside as well...you know.'

'Yes,' I said, 'I know.'

And yet. Gentle, loving—but always remote, and at the centre of her something unreachable. I remembered something I hadn't thought of for years, a day when we had taken a kite to fly high on the Yorkshire moors over Blackstone Edge. A day full of sun and wind and flying clouds. My mother running like a girl with her hair streaming and her face lit with laughter. Myself delirious with happiness because she was unbelievably, wonderfully sharing herself with me. And then her stopping, all at once, the light dying from her.

'Why did she do it?' Mary asked soberly. 'Why did she run off? In all these years, I've never been able to understand that.'

'She must have had some good reason.'

'And I've no doubt she found justification for it. We always do for the things we want to do, don't we? But whether it was good enough...your grandmother has never got over it. Lydia was the apple of her eye, there never was a child so loved. When she ran away—Mrs Stonor, well, it was just as if somebody took the sun from her. For a while after, it seemed to be all Richard, but it was never the same. It was like there was a cold inside her that nothing could warm—until Lois began to grow up into the very spit of Lydia.'

This threw a new light on the relationship between my mother and grandmother. We often hurt most the ones we love best. My mother herself had often said that, with what meaning I was now beginning to understand. Perhaps if she had stayed, the breach might have been healed. As it was, time and distance had intervened and stiffened old resentments, until in the end nothing could mend matters.

'What about her other daughter? What about Ellen?'

'Well, she was already dead then, wasn't she? That's what it was all about.'

'Was it? I don't know. I wish to heaven I did, but nobody will tell me—what *happened*, Mary?'

'Is that the truth you're telling me? You

don't know? Lydia kept it to herself all these years? Ah well, yes, it stands to reason she would.'

'She may have told my father, but I'm not sure she did. He never had any time for stupid family feuds and I'm sure he would have done something about persuading her to patch it up.'

Mary leaned over and pulled the plug out of its socket, then paused in the act of folding up the ironing board to give me a thoughtful look. 'It was a whole lot more than any family feud. And I'm not sure Lydia wasn't right. There's only your grandmother left now who knows the whole story, and maybe it's better that way.'

'You can't leave it like that!' I was on tiptoe with frustration, but Mary McDermott had pressed her lips firmly together and I saw that she wasn't to be moved.

'No,' she said, she didn't know the entire truth of it anyway, and it wasn't for her to go telling what she did know. And with a gleam of humour, she added, 'I'll not be giving herself the chance to say I've been encouraging you to gossip backstairs...where are you off to?'

'I'm going to make my grandmother tell me.'

'Do you imagine she will?'

'She must—she has to.'

'You're wasting your time. Nobody makes her do anything.'

But I ignored her half-exasperated warning as I raced breakneck up the stairs again.

Yet halfway up I came to a halt, struck by a thought the last few minutes had planted in my mind. On the landing, covering most of the walls, was a collection of family portraits. Centred between several of Lois as a child, placed at the head of the staircase so that it faced you as you came up, was a large photograph, coloured and blown up, of her parents, Richard and Dorothea. It was easy to see where Lois got her beauty. Richard had been a possessor of those Stonor good looks too, plus laughing eyes and a full quota of charm that leaped out at you even from the formal posed photograph. I felt I might have liked Richard. He looked the sort one did like, despite their faults, and there was a hint of weakness, a softness about him that suggested he might have had plenty. Poor Richard! His wife Dorothea didn't look very forbearing, a cool, pale blonde with smooth hair in the style of thirty-odd years ago and a plummy mouth, small and tucked in even when smiling in the photograph. A smile that didn't reach her eyes.

But search as I would, I could see no photograph of either my mother or Ellen. Ellen, whose death all those years ago had had something to do with my mother's flight.

The fact sank like a stone into my consciousness, and settled. I think I admitted then that Isabella might have some reason other than mere obstinacy for not wanting me to know what had happened. This was something that went deeper than a mere quarrel, something so much bigger that it had affected more lives than my mother's and Isabella's—and maybe still could. If my grandmother intended me ever to know, she would have told me already.

Yet my mother had sent me here. Indirectly, it was true, but that was always her way. I couldn't begin to fathom her reasons—but neither could I break faith with her.

4

It was gently peaceful, sitting on the grass under tall trees in Harvard Yard, which wasn't a yard in the English sense of the word but a quadrangle, a quiet expanse of tree-shaded grass surrounded by college buildings, intersected by paths busy with students. The white-painted spire of the brick Memorial Church soared into a sky cloudless and blue as a starling's egg.

'I've brought lunch with me—might as well have it now,' Harmony announced, unwrapping the delicatessen paper bag she held. 'Submarines. Hope you like pastrami.' She handed me a ten-inch long roll, split down the middle and overflowing with sliced sausages, cooked meats and pickles, a paper napkin I was surely going to need, and a can of root beer.

'Thanks. I see you're back on your diet.' Dividing my roll, I put the other half back in the bag.

'Oh, that!' She wrinkled her nose, adjusting the gold-rimmed spectacles that constantly slipped down it. 'Time to start reducing when finals are over.' What was visible of her pretty face behind the specs and the hair lit up in a grin. 'And that is positively my last word about work today. It's all so iffy, anyway. So—'

'Go on.'

'No, it doesn't matter. Charlotte, please—don't go putting on that expression and start getting all English and stuffy with me. I'm going to be good today, right?'

I saw she had made an effort to appear less freaked-out than usual. There wasn't a lot she could do about her hair, outgrowing its Wash n'Wear twelve dollars fifty permanent and sticking out around her face like an old-fashioned rag doll's, but instead of the collection of Oxfam rejects she normally affected her not-so-plump-as-she-thought figure was clad in a decent shirt and a clean pair of Levis. 'Haven't I already told you I think you're mad to give up your course? So there's no point in repeating myself. But have you talked to Max yet?'

'No,' she admitted, pulling a face and licking ketchup from her fingers. 'Thought I'd be diplomatic and wait until we're at the Point. He's always more relaxed there.'

She didn't seem to think it might be different this year, that going back to the scene of his wife's death might affect even Max's cool self-control. 'Grandmother *is* going this year—she hasn't let Rowena persuade her out of it?'

I shook my head and told her what had happened earlier. 'Bully for her,' she said. 'You'll really like the Point. It's so different from here in Boston. Gosh, I hate all that rich scene up on the Hill.' Then suddenly, 'When I do talk to Max, I'd really appreciate it if you'd be there also, Charlotte.'

'Me?'

Between Harmony and myself instant friendship had sprung up. We had taken to each other immediately, by-passing most of the preliminaries so that although we had only met a few times it was as though we had known each other for years. Even so, I thought this was asking a bit much. 'Why me? I thought Max was your father confessor.'

'A-ha, you're scared of him!'

'No. Only terrified.'

'Oh, don't take any notice of all that ice-man stuff. It doesn't mean anything when you get to know him. He's always been marvellous with me, especially when I was a kid, after my parents...but sometimes, he can be so *off*-putting. You know.'

Only too well I knew, but in the end, reluctantly, I agreed. If that was what she wanted, I'd be there when she approached Max. 'But not if you want me to add my support—because I think you're wrong.'

'Just be there, Charlotte, hm?'

I let it go. She seemed uncharacteristically on edge today. Some of her fizz was missing. Once or twice she seemed about to say something else, then stopped. For the umpteenth time she took a surreptitious peep over her shoulder. 'Sure you don't want this?' she asked finally, demolishing the last crumbs of her submarine sandwich and picking up the other half of mine.

'Go ahead. You can have my root beer, too.'

'You don't like it!' Her face registered amazement.

'It wouldn't leave an unstoppable gap in my life if I never tasted it again...the sandwich was delicious.'

'Well, just give me a chance to finish it off, then I guess we'd better be making tracks, if we're going to take in Bunker Hill and all.'

Thoughtfully, I stared at a group of students lolling on the steps of the Memorial Church. Was that why she had brought me here, simply to enlist my support when facing Max, giving up a day to do so at a time which was so crucial for her? Despite her stated desire to give up her course, she had been swotting hard; it was one thing to leave college with a good record behind you, quite another to leave after you had failed. Boston and its history would still be there when her exams were over, and she knew I wasn't planning to return home before then.

'Why Cassie, hello!'

'Hi, Harmony.'

A young woman with a large undisciplined figure moulded into tight trousers and a mercifully loose top stood in front of us, hung about with parcels, a lot of jewellery, a bulging handbag and a big, floppy-brimmed hat.

'Charlotte,' Harmony said, a little breathlessly, 'I want you to meet my friend Cassie Hayter. Cassie, here is Charlotte, my cousin from England.'

'Hi, Charlotte, I've heard about you.'

Cassie plonked herself down on the grass beside us, sagged and loosed her hold on her belongings, letting them subside in a tide around her. 'Boy, am I beat! I just loathe shopping. I guess I'm too soft-hearted, they can persuade me into buying anything.' She had small, sharp brown eyes, a lot more alert than the rest of her. 'Well of course, I know what it's like, don't I?'

I threw her a mystified glance, but she was looking at Harmony. Harmony said nothing, and Cassie turned back to me. 'I should've taken you with me, Charlotte, to help me choose. That blouse you're wearing, it's neat!' She sighed rapturously over my unextraordinary print blouse.

'Well, thanks.'

'You're not a bit what I expected, for goodness sake.'

I thought about several replies to that one. I said weakly, 'Oh, do you really think so?'

'And I just *love* your English accent!'

I could hardly see our acquaintance ripening into a mutually satisfying relationship if the conversation were to continue at this level, and I felt Harmony, unusually silent, might have done more to help it along. Strange, because I had had the distinct impression she'd been glad to see Cassie when she appeared on the scene. Almost as if she'd been expecting her. Cassie was considerably older than Harmony, close on thirty, I guessed, and seemed an odd sort of chum for her. She went on exclaiming over my make-up, my hair, my accent, giving Harmony occasional meaning looks to which she didn't respond. Eventually, with a regretful sigh, she began gathering up the flotsam around her. 'It's been great meeting you, Charlotte, but I should be on my way. I've a long drive back and there's no profit in a closed shop...Harmony's told you about my little business?'

'Not yet,' Harmony said quickly.

'Oh?' Cassie's eyes flickered. Then she laughed, indulgently. 'My, Harmony, you're such a little scatterbrain, aren't you?' Harmony shot her a look which held something very sharp in it, then looked at the grass. 'Well, I have this boutique, Charlotte, up on the coast, where I sell jewellery that I make myself.'

'Like that pendant you're wearing?'

'This? Oh, sure.' She lifted the pendant from where, small and dainty, it bobbed incongruously up and down on her ample bosom. 'It's made from wampum.'

I fished around amongst half-memories of long ago lessons on North America. Pemmican, Hiawatha, wampum... 'That's Indian, isn't it?'

Cassie's eyes widened with unflattering surprise. 'Clever of you! Yes, wampum beads are what the Algonquian Indians used to use for money. It's actually the inside of the quahog clam shell. Like it?'

'It's beautifully made.' I leaned forward to take a closer look at the polished violet-coloured shell, charmingly set in filigree silver, turning the pendant with a sense of dé-jà vu. 'They certainly don't come prettier.'

'If you like that sort of thing,' said Harmony, who never wore jewellery.

'Why, Harmony, it's a real good-selling line, not as expensive as the semi-precious stones I do, but people like things with associations. I sell other things as well, Charlotte, mostly for the tourist trade—woodwork, weaving, anything that's genuinely hand-crafted. I guess I'm lucky to have a pool of very capable people who supply me. This summer I'm expecting to do a very good turnover—but isn't that life? That's the very thing that's putting me in a real fix...I make my jewellery in back of my shop, you see, and I can't cope too well with serving customers and all, on my own.'

I looked at Harmony. She was sitting hugging her knees, still looking down at the grass.

'That's really why I'm here today,' Cassie went on, fixing me with a stare. Her eyes looked like hard, shiny brown beads. 'I've been seeing someone with a view to getting fixed up with a partner, if only she would make her mind up, then I can afford to have someone mind the shop. But you can only push so far, if you're sensitive, like me.' She sighed, heaved herself to her feet, gathered her scattered belongings. 'Now I *have* to go. It's been a real privilege meeting you, Charlotte. You'll call me, won't you, Harmony? See you.'

It was Harmony who broke the silence after she'd gone. 'You all set, too? If you are, let's go. I have the car parked not too far away.'

'Wow!' she exclaimed, four hours later, wiping her brow with an exaggerated gesture as we stood on the deck of the old frigate *Constitution*. 'And there's still Bunker Hill to do.'

From where we stood could be seen the impressive granite column of the monument commemorating the famous battle with the English, standing on its hill reputed to have nearly three hundred steps to the top. 'Not today there isn't,' I told her firmly, leaning on the brass rail and trying to take the weight off my feet. 'I've had as much history and as many museums as I can take.'

Most of the afternoon had been spent in meeting houses where spirited colonial gentlemen, two hundred years before, had sworn allegiance to the cause of personal freedom. We had examined relics of war, documents, models of battlefields. We had visited the spot where outraged citizens had tipped chests of precious tea into the harbour rather than pay the exorbitant taxes demanded by their mother country. We had seen an allegedly real pinch of that tea. We were standing now on the deck of the nicknamed "Old Ironsides" which had never lost a fight.

'It's been interesting, though?' Harmony queried.

'Marvellous—it's just that I've got mental indigestion, and probably fallen arches as well.'

'Poor you—but I'm happy you enjoyed it. I really wanted you to.'

'And you wanted me to meet Cassie as well, didn't you? It was no accident that we met, was it?'

There was a pause.

'Goodness, that wasn't why—well, not entirely...I—I did think it a good opportunity...'

She stared over the rails down into the murky waters of the Navy shipyard, as absorbed as if it were the translucent Caribbean, where tropical fish and coral reefs might sprout below. A yellow school bus with "Manchester" inscribed on its side in large letters drew up alongside, disgorging a horde of twenty or thirty children, armed with notebooks and pencils. The young attendants on the ship, disguised as sometime sailors in striped jerseys and shiny black boaters, suddenly sprang to life as small boys and girls streaked up the gangplanks, disappeared down the hatches, swung on the highly polished Liberty bell, and general pandemonium broke out.

'Hey, you kids!' A voice called the children to order, without noticeable result, but eventually whoever was in charge managed to gather them together and direct them below decks.

In the comparative quiet that followed, I said, 'You should have told me the truth, that why you wanted to leave college was to go in with Cassie in her business. Especially if you want me on your side, Max too, to persuade your grandmother it would be a good thing.'

'Nobody can stop me,' she began defensively, turning back to her contemplation of the water. 'If I want to quit—'

'I don't suppose they can, but you won't, will you? Not without Isabella's blessing. Because then you wouldn't get the money that Cassie needs?'

The Stars and Stripes above the rigging flapped smartly, like washing in a stiff breeze. Harmony swung round and stared at me, her face bright pink.

'It isn't like that at all—you've got me so wrong! Grandmother is my legal guardian, with Max, for another year, and they have control of my money, sure, and I know she can be difficult and all, but I don't come in for *her* money, why should I? It isn't as though I'm a Stonor. Oh,' she went on, seeing my blank expression, with a small cynical smile that wasn't like her, 'I see nobody's filled you out on the details. Nobody's told you I'm not one of the elect, have they?'

So then she told me what I hadn't known, that Richard Stonor hadn't been her father, that he and her mother Dorothea had both previously been married to someone else, and subsequently divorced.

'I—see. Then Lois wasn't your sister?'

'Gosh, no! But Richard didn't let it make any difference, not ever. He always treated me as his own daughter, he was just—great. I really loved him, you know? Would you believe it was my mother who never had any time for me? She was much closer to Lois... I guess she'd found a readymade daughter, nearly grown up and without all the hassle of raising her, not like the fiend of a kid I was. They really related to each other, into clothes, make-up and all that.'

Her casual, off-hand manner couldn't conceal the childish jealousy of the older, sophisticated girl who had usurped her in her mother's life, the still-present hurt, the deep and lasting feeling of rejection. It said a lot about Harmony's present attitudes, her clothes, her preferred lifestyle...

'When they died, Richard and my

mother, it was the worst time of my entire life. Except for one other time,' she qualified, pausing before adding: 'He was my true father. My other father, I don't even know if he exists still.'

'How old were you then—when Richard died?'

'Ten. Lois was nearly fourteen years older.'

'Old enough to take care of you.'

'Lois? That's a laugh. She was never aware I even existed. Besides, she was only just married to Max, that was still new. *He* was different, though. If it hadn't been for him...'

Leaning against the rail, she told me how it had been, about Richard and how he had legally adopted her and changed her name, though even that hadn't apparently made any difference to Isabella, as far as inheriting the Stonor fortune went. 'My blood just isn't blue enough. I have a bit of capital that Dad—Richard—left me, though. In actual fact, quite a lot,' she amended defiantly, as if it were something to be ashamed of. 'But money isn't important, as long as you use it right. If I can help Cassie along...she's very talented, you know.' She avoided looking at me.

'Well,' I said after a minute, doing my best to remain unprejudiced, 'It's your cash. But do you have to put yourself into the business along with it? Can't you just wait until you've graduated, at least?

She caught her breath, and several emotions chased each other across her face. Alarm, wariness, doubt. Most of all doubt. 'I—I don't know, I'm not certain of anything. Anyway, it can't be bad, to try something new, to get away. This last year hasn't been too hot.'

I asked carefully, 'Because of Colin?'

The look she turned on me was curiously blank and opaque. I felt a withdrawing from me, a closing up. Then she said casually, but with unexpected finality, 'Don't, Charlotte. All that was over before you came here, and it isn't possible you can understand—in any way whatsoever.'

It was an impulse of pure curiosity that made me cross the road when I saw the sign, but it was some deeper instinct that caused me to push open the door and walk up the stairs. I wasn't in need of refreshment, since I'd just had a tall glass of ice-cold orange juice with Harmony, sitting on a bench in the jazzed-up, stylishly colourful Quincy Market area. When we had parted company she had driven back to Cambridge, but I had preferred to walk back up to Beacon Hill. I wanted to think about several aspects of my talk with her, and our meeting with Cassie Hayter.

I hardly noticed where I was going until all at once I became aware I'd taken a wrong turning, maybe several. And there it was, across the road, Rowena's Place, flamboyantly asserting itself. Maybe I hadn't chanced upon the spot, maybe I'd been fated to find myself there.

What I had expected from the sign outside I don't know, something flashy and ornate maybe, but not what it turned out to be. The restaurant floor was reached by a flight of dark, narrow steps, and the wide, light-filled space as you emerged was either a stroke of luck, or a piece of design precisely calculated to impress. Whichever it was, it succeeded. The whole of one wall was window, with a view right across the harbour, and the opposite wall was mirror glass reflecting ocean and sky so that wherever you sat you were likely to have a magnificent view. Terrific, day or night.

The place was empty of customers at

that hour, but Rowena was there, doing accounts at a corner of the small bar. She looked up and saw me when I came in, and if she was surprised she didn't show it. But then she didn't show any pleasure, either. Thin and immaculate in her crisp white suit, she put down her pen and came from behind the bar to greet me, ushered me to a table and insisted on having coffee and Danish pastries brought.

'You're having some too, Rowena?'

'A cup of coffee, maybe.'

I looked round more closely while we were waiting for it to arrive. When Rowena had chosen her decor, she had had the sense to keep it simple. The two walls were stone-coloured, the floor coverings a neutral cord, the tables and chairs bamboo. The natural scene outside did the rest.

'This is lovely,' I told her.

She gave an indifferent shrug. Indifferent to what she had created or to my opinion wasn't clear. No amount of compliments, however sincere, could make my cousin Rowena open up and be friendly.

I had seen her every time she visited Isabella, several times a week since my arrival in Boston, but I was no nearer being friends with her than I was at our first meeting, when she had faced me with open hostility. Not that I blamed her entirely, that time. She had known nothing about me, or my expected arrival; had been unaware of my very existence until then, when Isabella had introduced me to her, a fait accompli. Since then she had kept a guard on herself whenever we met, though I didn't flatter myself it was due to any nice regard for my feelings. More likely, she simply didn't want to antagonise Isabella any more than necessary.

She watched me warily now as I sipped my coffee, evidently wondering when I was going to get to the point of my being there. I was beginning to grow embarrassed under that suspicious scrutiny, to search around for an excuse to offer—I hadn't after all ever been invited here—when Sebastian walked in.

Being glad to see Sebastian Garth was a new experience. Raising his hand in greeting, he went to the bar and poured himself a generous drink before coming across to us.

'This is a pleasant surprise. Welcome to Rowena's Place, cousin Charlotte.'

Lifting his glass, he knocked back two-thirds of the contents before bending to kiss Rowena, moving impatiently back as finickily she twitched an almost invisible piece of fluff from his lapel. No cousinly kiss this time for me to avoid, though his greeting was warm enough. But Sebastian's warmth was always something I distrusted.

'What do you think,' he asked patronisingly, 'of Ro's little venture?' Pulling a chair out and leaning back in it, twisting his lips in that wry smile. 'Any time now I'm about to retire and let her keep me in the style to which I'm accustomed.'

Rowena's gaze became a little fixed. Sebastian's smile broadened. I repeated my favourable opinion of the restaurant.

'It might even bring in money one day,' he said.

Rowena was quick on the defensive. 'Of course it will, given time.'

'A lot of time, a lot of luck.'

'And hard work. There isn't any other way to get rich.'

Between them passed a look, defiance on her part, on his something akin to malice. Her eyes followed his deliberately careful return to the bar to follow up his drink, which hadn't been his first or his second recently, her fingers unconsciously smoothing down the tablecloth, setting the cruet dead centre. Isabella had been right to suspect that Sebastian hadn't relished Rowena sinking her inheritance into this business. There had been a barbed cruelty under his words that I didn't like. Not for the first time, I reflected on the advantages of having no money to speak of. And I experienced a flash of unexpected sympathy with Rowena. 'You must have worked very hard already,' I remarked.

She spread her hands, shrugging, but Sebastian, resuming his seat, put in ironically, 'Oh, she worked hard, believe me. You should have seen it when she bought it. Before she would even sit down and look what had to be done, she actually scrubbed it down herself from top to bottom.' His words mocked Rowena's fastidiousness, but I fancied I wasn't wrong in detecting a reluctant respect lurking behind them.

Rowena was tapping non-existent ash off her cigarette. I tried to imagine those slender, delicate white hands wielding a scrubbing brush, and totally failed. 'That's right,' she said, reading my expression and giving me one of her rare smiles. 'I'm not such an unlikely candidate for Isabella's granddaughter as you may imagine. I can go all out for what I want, too.'

She had almost made a joke. It struck me that Rowena might be a much more complicated person than she appeared; in other circumstances, we might have got on. Now, all her defences were out against me. She had already shrugged off the possible moment of rapport, and Sebastian was asking me what had brought me to the restaurant, the questions she had been too polite, or too uncaring, to put. I told him how I had found myself in the vicinity, after spending the day with Harmony. I also mentioned the meeting with Cassie Hayter.

'Do you know her?' I asked.

'Oh, I—' began Rowena, but Sebastian intervened.

'We hardly move in student circles, cousin Charlotte.'

'She isn't a student—she didn't seem Harmony's type at all. In fact, I thought her—weird.' Sebastian flicked me a look that noticed my involuntary shrinking. I went on with an uneasy laugh, 'Silly, I was almost going to say, dangerous.' Silly it might have been, and I hadn't been conscious of feeling that way about Cassie until I said it, but yes, she was a dangerous woman, I was sure. Unscrupulous, the sort who wouldn't hesitate a moment over the means she used to get what she wanted.

'Dangerous?' Sebastian repeated softly. 'Why do you think that?'

'I don't know—but, well, doesn't Harmony have rather a lot of money, for one thing?'

There was a glint of some expression in his eyes that I couldn't immediately put a name to, but it was one I didn't like. 'Yes,' he said, 'she has.' Then he yawned. He was a man who bored easily, if the subject didn't immediately concern himself. 'It isn't worth upsetting yourself over. Harmony gets into these involvements from time to time. It won't last.'

I wasn't prepared to argue that. I was a stranger to the whole set-up here, and though Harmony appeared so transparent on the surface it took longer than three weeks to know about someone. I said, changing the subject, 'You asked this morning if Isabella had mentioned Stonor's Point to me. She spoke to me after you left. She's already begun to make preparations.'

Rowena set the coffee pot down, very carefully, very precisely. 'I might have known,' she said at last. 'She always wins.' Then to me, 'Think yourself lucky. You'll be back in England by then, won't you?'

'I've promised her I'll stay for a while. Actually, I'm very much looking forward to seeing the house.'

I knew immediately I spoke that I had said much more than merely announcing my delayed return home. A chilly dislike began to permeate the atmosphere. Neither looked directly at me. I could feel my motives being questioned...but though they might suspect, they couldn't know what Isabella was hoping and planning for my future. And I thought it was just as well.

'Max seems to think it won't do her any harm,' I said.

'Then good luck to her.' Despite her obvious effort at self-control, Rowena's hand shook as she reached towards the pack of cigarettes on the table and helped herself. Her voice began to rise unsteadily. 'I hope she enjoys sitting there celebrating Grandfather Ralph's birthday with a company of ghosts for houseguests. Just so long as we don't have to be there.'

'Easy, Ro, easy now. Don't upset yourself. All that's past and gone. Forget it.'

Unhurriedly, Sebastian reached his hand out and covered hers. It looked like reassurance. It seemed to me to be a warning. Rowena was obviously working herself into a state where she might say things she would later regret.

'Ghosts, you say? Whose ghosts? Ezekiel Stonor and his bride?'

My attempt at levity was met without humour. Removing her hand from Sebastian's and half turning from him, Rowena said shakily, 'We have other ghosts at Stonor's Point. My mother, my grandfather...Lois. And I for one can't face a repetition of last year, with Grandmother practically insisting it was—' She bit off the words, her face drained of colour.

My antennae were quivering in earnest now. 'Was what?'

'Forget it,' she said sharply, clearly annoyed at her own indiscretion, but Sebastian couldn't let an opportunity like that pass.

'Murder, cousin Charlotte,' he said, tipping his chair on to its back legs.

'Murder?' The light curtains at the window near the bar bellied inwards in a spiteful gust of wind from the sea. The impossible word hung in the silence. 'You can't be serious. Why should she imagine anyone would want to do that?'

'Speaking truthfully,' he drawled, his gaze on the ceiling, 'because any one of us might have. Any damn one of us. Though I could name you one or two outside the family who wouldn't have been sorry to see Lois Remmick out of the way also—'

'What kind of talk is that?' Rowena interrupted.

'Straight talk, Ro my love. Cousin Charlotte is one of the family now. She should know how honest we all are.'

Ignoring his sarcasm, she said, 'I wasn't being fair. I shouldn't have said anything. Grandmother wasn't—herself, when she said that. She never was quite sane where Lois was concerned and now, at her age...she mustn't go back! You have to stop her, Charlotte.'

'I? You really believe I have any influence over her?' I almost laughed.

But it was Rowena who laughed, short and nervous. 'Haven't you? Lois could always twist Isabella round her little finger.'

'You're forgetting. I'm not Lois.'

Sebastian cleared his throat.

I saw now how wrong, how naïve I had

been in thinking, a moment ago, that they didn't know what Isabella was up to. They knew all right, because they knew Isabella, better than I did. They knew I'd been selected as Lois's successor. Waves of hostility—no, hatred—washed towards me, so tangible that I shrank. I remembered what I'd said to Max—that whether or not Isabella seriously believed I would accept her offer was immaterial, the point being that I was there, odds-on favourite for the moment, to keep them on their toes. The malicious enjoyment derived from watching them seethe with jealousy was all she wanted.

Feeling the strength of their animosity towards me, it wasn't too easy to appreciate that sort of irony.

And in view of what had just been said, I wondered if there wasn't something else to take account of, something still more frightening. If Isabella did indeed believe that Lois might have been murdered, and I was understood to have taken her place in the scheme of things, wasn't I being set up as the perfect decoy duck to flush out the murderer? If Lois had been killed to remove her from the succession, that is, and not for some other reason. Was that an additional motive behind Isabella's actions?

I would have liked to think that she believed this hypothetical murderer would reveal himself in some other way than by making a second attempt, if so. But I was beginning to wonder if Rowena's accusation had been as wild as it seemed, or if truly there were areas where my grandmother wasn't wholly in command of herself.

5

The traffic was escalating into the evening rush as I left the restaurant to make my way back to my grandmother's house. Crossing one of the busy main roads to the halfway traffic island, waiting for the lights to change, standing there amongst the everyday bustle of shopping crowds and homegoing workers, what had just passed seemed suddenly quite crazy, hysterically manufactured by Rowena, egged on by Sebastian.

Four lanes of cars swung round the bend in the road and came on down the straight like the last lap at Monaco; behind me the crowd built up as I waited.

The conversation with the two of them had all the same left a cold lump inside me, uneasy as undigested food. And inexplicably, the unease began to grow as I stood there watching the red light. All at once, I felt chokingly hemmed in, threatened. I tried to turn, but because of the press of people behind I couldn't even manage to look over my shoulder. Fear was there, right behind me. I felt it pressing closer, pushing at me. I willed myself to stay upright, but for the life of me I couldn't. I was falling, right into the path of the traffic.

It was the jaywalker who saved me. Darting across to the accompaniment of a blare of horns and screeching brakes, he skipped smartly in front of a scarlet monster and fetched up smack in front of me just as I toppled, shoving me and those behind me back in order to get his foothold on the island. His whole weight came against me, the crowd gave way and I staggered back, my ankle twisting sickeningly.

The lights changed, the jaywalker lost himself again in the next influx of pedestrians, and the crowd round me surged across, except for one or two concerned strangers who wanted to know if I was unhurt... 'Oughta be some control of the numbers on these here islands!'... 'Guys like him, he could've caused a real pile-up.'...

'You sure you can walk now, honey?' a kindly woman asked.

Gingerly, I tested my ankle. 'I think so,

thanks. Yes, I'm fine. No bones broken.' Another set of people were now pressing around us, and I prepared to hobble to the other side at the next lights change.

Then a voice I knew. 'What's the trouble there? Anyone hurt?'

The crowd parted like the Red Sea for Max Remmick. An initial exclamation at seeing me, a hurried explanation by my kind friend, and somehow he had managed to get me to the other side of the road and ordered me to stay where I was until he had fetched his car from where it was parked around the corner. 'I'll be with you as quick as I can.'

I leaned shakily against the plate-glass window of a department store displaying cruisewear in hot, dazzling colours, until I saw the navy-blue Pontiac draw into the kerb. Before Max could get out I had the passenger door open and had climbed in beside him.

'Shouldn't think there's much wrong if you can move like that,' he remarked dryly, starting up.

'No, I don't suppose it's more than a wrench.'

I was rewarded with an austere look. 'More than likely, but it will still need looking at when we get you home. How did it happen? That woman wasn't very coherent.'

I explained briefly, leaving out the real reason why I'd almost fallen to my death in front of those speeding cars. I could imagine his reaction if I told him the truth: somebody in that crowd tried to kill me. Somebody pressed forward so hard that I would be bound to fall. He would laugh, or look at me with that scornful expression he could so easily assume...though hadn't he himself warned me, last night, that I might find I had enemies? It was a new and unwelcome thought that there were people who disliked and resented me. But still I hesitated to elaborate. Had I felt the actual thrust of hands at my back? In retrospect, I wouldn't have been prepared to swear to anything except that powerful feeling of danger.

He listened attentively enough, but when I'd finished all he said was, 'People panic too easily,' in a remote, disapproving sort of voice, as if his mind was concentrating on something else. Obviously, well-conducted persons, like Max Remmick, didn't allow themselves to have humiliating public accidents.

‘It could have been very nasty,’ I pointed out, nettled.

‘Must be your lucky day, then.’

‘As it is, I should have had a very uncomfortable time getting home...quite a coincidence, you being on hand, wasn’t it? Right on the spot where it happened.’

‘Not really. I’d taken time off to shop for a birthday present for my niece.’ He jerked his head to the back seat, where a large gift-wrapped parcel reposed. I didn’t remember seeing him carrying it when he’d rescued me, but then I’d had other things to bother me. ‘I was on my way home when I spotted you. I came after you to offer you a ride, but I lost sight of you.’

Still. If anyone likely to have occasion to wish me harm had wormed his way into the crowd behind me, it had to be someone known to him also, therefore he would surely have seen him...wouldn’t he? Not necessarily. The crowd had been very thick, and he had said he lost sight of me. I was becoming as neurotic as Rowena. My near fall had been a natural panic reaction at the thought of all those people pushing forward. Or a subconscious fear of the enemies he had spoken of? Or one of those enemies actually ill-wishing me?

A cold finger of dismay seemed to stroke the back of my neck. I wasn't sure whether I preferred to believe that, or that danger had been there in person.

'What,' Isabella demanded, 'has happened?'

'Don't get alarmed. Some hot sweet tea for Charlotte, Mary.'

Ignoring my protests, Max helped me into the house, supporting me with his arm and leading me into his own room, Isabella following.

'It's nothing to make a fuss about,' I said.

'Who's fussing?' He settled me in a chair, pulled up a long stool on which to rest my leg, unstrapped my sandal and began his examination. I averted my eyes from the unpleasing sight of my bare toes, grubby with an afternoon's sightseeing, looking even grubbier against his well-scrubbed, well-manicured hands, his pristine shirt cuffs with their gold links. There were golden hairs to match along the backs of his hands. I sipped obediently at the scalding orange tea Mary had brought. It was not at all nice, setting my teeth on edge with its unaccustomed, unpalatable sweetness and strength.

'Nothing much the matter there,' Max announced presently, 'but you'd be wise to rest it for a day or two. I'll strap it up.'

'It won't prevent her going to the Point?' Isabella cried at once, anxiety overcoming tact.

'Of course it won't.' He went in search of his bag while Isabella, ceasing to hover, sat down and demanded an explanation.

'And what were you doing at Rowena's place of business?' she asked, as Max returned and began competently to work an elastic support over my foot. His head jerked up.

'Oh? You didn't tell me you'd been there,' he said sharply. He was still in that disagreeable, impatient mood which I found so difficult. Why should it have been necessary to tell him?

'I was passing. I thought I'd show an interest.

'Very laudable,' Isabella remarked dryly. 'Taking the opportunity, no doubt, to discuss with her how this poor old woman can be prevented from her own foolish actions, such as going to Stonor's Point?'

'On the contrary. I told them you were going ahead with your plans and had no intention of being stopped.'

'Hmph,' she said, but I could see she was pleased at this; she could even afford to smile as she informed Max that I was going to be there, too.

'I shall be able to keep an eye on you, then.'

Professionally, or otherwise he didn't say. His tone had given nothing away, but as he finished adjusting the support he raised his head. Our eyes met and unexpectedly, like a shock, something passed between us. A look, a spark, some empathy, and a stillness as his look held mine. A slow dawning smile that took the impatient frown away and made him appear years younger, so that one saw he was a very attractive man, in a way that had nothing to do with good looks.

'You'll like it there,' he said. 'Do you swim? Do you like boats?'

'Swimming yes, I love it. I've never done any sailing.'

'Sailing?' he repeated, and Isabella laughed.

'That's too slow for Max. His passion is speed.'

Yes, I could believe that. He would like to move fast. 'Well, I like speed, too.'

'You do? Then I'll have to take you out in my speedboat. I'll be up there for the birthday, and driving down as many weekends as I can through the summer.' He slipped my sandal on again and carefully fastened it. 'What small feet you have,' he remarked, tweaking one of my toes, and stood up. 'You'll live now.'

The idea of Stonor's Point apparently cast no shadow over him. Either he was a cold frog who didn't really care that his wife had died there—and one could very easily at times believe that of Max Remmick—or he was in total command of his emotions, which was refreshing after the hysteria the very mention of the place seemed to conjure up in everyone else. As I stood up I took stock of the room, impersonal as a waiting-room. After the superfluity of photos of Lois in the rest of the house, it was strange to find not one of her in her husband's room.

Max's hours were erratic and long. He often ate alone, late at night, and went straight to his rooms, but he managed to take time off his busy schedule to drive Isabella and Mary McDermott to Stonor's Point. Harmony and I followed in her little orange Japanese car. Either second thoughts or Sebastian had prevailed, because Rowena had also decided to be there, at least until after the birthday celebration was over, and had driven up earlier.

We sped along the road out of Boston. A lake alongside the highway glittered in the sun, feathery sumach trees which would turn scarlet in the autumn swayed as we swooshed past. Harmony drove with dash and verve and a dislike of anything in front of her, humming under her breath. I too was lighthearted, irrationally convinced that Stonor's Point must give me the answer to the enigma of my mother's flight. The exhilarating speed of the car intensified our cheerfulness and made me remember Max's promise to take me out in his speedboat.

The road was busy with weekend traffic and Harmony hugged the back of the family station wagon sedately occupying the fast lane. When at last the driver got the message and she was able to pass it and put her foot down again on the empty stretch of freeway in front of us, she said impatiently, 'These roads are kind of boring. How about making a detour and driving through the countryside and along the coast road? It won't be quick, but at least it's pretty.'

I was surprised, but agreed we were in no hurry, and after we left the highway at the next exit she slowed down, allowing me to enjoy the sweet and gentle countryside. New England towns and villages came and went, bathed in golden sunlight, small and elm-shaded, with names from Old England, like Andover, Wakefield, Reading. White-steepled meeting houses and churches stood on village greens, prosperous white-frame houses were set well back from the road amongst more elms and maple. Spacious, orderly, well-brushed, like a picture on a calendar.

I could tell Harmony was pleased that I liked it so much. 'Oh, but wait until you see it in the fall,' she said with a proprietary air. 'The colours are really something then.'

She too was assuming, like Isabella, that I would still be here, but I kept my thoughts to myself.

We crossed the wide Merrimack river. As we drew near the coast the air subtly changed. The signposts began to read Ipswich, Essex, Gloucester. Creeks and inlets jutted right into towns thronged with fishing boats and pleasure yachts. Harmony pointed out old clapboard houses with railed widows' walks on the roofs, where sea captains' wives used to keep vigil for homebound vessels, reminder of the towns' origins as fishing and whaling ports.

Sniffing the air, she said, 'Hm. The sea smell always makes me hungry.'

'Not again!'

'I know a place where we can get some delicious seafood.'

We pulled into O'Grady's Diner, ate some clams and shrimp salad, then turned along the twisting coast road which soon became more rugged, more deserted, with only an occasional spacious property facing the beach.

'Not long now,' Harmony announced. 'Another few miles and we'll be there.' She shot me an oblique look. 'We're not too far from Cassie's shop. Maybe we should stop off and see it.'

'If you like.'

'We can turn off just along here. The road makes a loop and then rejoins the main road just short of Stonor's Point.'

A few minutes later we were driving into

a picturesque village which she explained was still a working fishing community, though it was now something of an artists' colony and a weekend sailing resort as well.

'Will you look at all these people!' Slowing down, she guided the car through the narrow twisting streets, jammed with visitors, cars parked nose to tail along its length. 'We'll never get through.'

'You're going to find it difficult to park even if you do.'

'That's okay. I know where to go.' We inched along the road, and eventually turned into a narrow alleyway and found a spot among some deserted backyards.

Cassie's boutique was one of a row of low, shingle-roofed, boarded cabins along the pier. A picture gallery called Miranda Martell, devoted to scenic representations of unimaginable crudity, stood on one side, an ice-cream parlour on the other. The shop was closed, with a notice on the door written in scarlet felt-tipped pen reading 'Back Soon'.

'This is how it is.' Harmony was evidently disappointed. 'If she has to go out, she has to shut up shop. There's no knowing what trade she misses.'

Most of the tourists in the street seemed to be more intent on taking snapshots than buying anything, and a glance around confirmed my guess that all these shops must duplicate each other with the goods they could offer. Maybe that didn't matter in the height of the season. It was crowded now. It would be like Blackpool prom then.

'I know where Cassie leaves the key, if you want to look inside. I don't suppose she'll be long, anyway, and it seems a pity...'

'Why not?'

She slipped into the art gallery next door while I waited, staring into Cassie's shop window, which was colourful and attractive. A small lamp burned in one corner, softly illuminating a collection of coloured glassware and some sea-shells, coral and dried seaweed artistically arranged on a drift of sand. Crotchetwork shawls, cheesecloth dresses and third-world cottons hung as a backcloth.

Brandishing the key, Harmony came back and unlocked the door, stepped inside and switched on a lamp or two. 'Voila, madame!'

It was darkish and cluttered inside, the

sort of clutter that is supposed to encourage customers to potter. Against a stripped pine dresser were displayed one or two small antiques, a Pennsylvania-Dutch painted chest, a collection of winsome Mary Gregory glass, some pieces of scrimshaw. Macrame and canework swung from the ceiling, holding a profusion of healthy green plants; one wall was devoted to shelves containing handthrown pottery glazed in a distinctive olive green and smoky purple. I *had* been doing Cassie an injustice, at least in assuming her shop to be as unprepossessing as her person.

'This is all Cassie's own work, over here.'

I went to join Harmony by a display case containing some astonishingly beautiful brooches and necklaces in amethyst, quartz and agate, set in shattered gold and chunky silver, alongside some of the delicate filigree-set wampum jewellery that Cassie herself wore.

'It's beautiful, isn't it?'

I had to agree, unreservedly. There was a very special talent here. The jewellery was original and quite exquisite, that was evident, without Harmony's rather desperate anxiety for my approval. 'Would you like to see where she makes it?' She held aside a bead curtain that screened the back premises.

'Yes, but you can stop acting as saleswoman of the year. I'm impressed. Cassie's made a marvellous job of the whole thing.'

She halted with the beads draped over her arm. 'To be honest, it isn't all Cassie's doing. She had a partner until quite recently. Looking after the shop was her part, the creative part was Cassie's. Here's where she works—her living-room's through there.'

The back of the shop was more what I had expected. Jewellery in various stages of completion littered most surfaces, an electric drum for polishing stones stood in one corner, tools lay scattered about, gold and silver chains hung from hooks on the wall. Most of the storage shelves were crazily untidy. An open jar of peanut butter stood on top of a large safe.

'Don't be put off by all this. It's really a very well-run business. Well worth investing in, wouldn't you say?'

I picked up a large, smoothly-rounded rock from the bench, cut like half a coconut to reveal an amazing pink crystalline centre, glowing as the pearly inside of a pomegranate. 'I want to help you, Harmony, really I do.'

'But you think I'm crazy, don't you?'

I didn't think she was crazy, or stupid, that was what worried me. She walked to the back window, rubbed a clean patch in its grime and stared out, hands deep in the pockets of her jeans, then swung round. 'I'm not just doing this for the fun of it, you know. It's important to me, you can't know how important.'

'In what way?'

'Because—well...' She frowned and said, 'I can't tell you. You'll just have to take my word that it is.'

I thought it possible we might go on indefinitely in this fashion. I was beginning to have my own ideas, or suspicions, and I said, 'You couldn't go into it without having everything thoroughly investigated, of course.'

Her eyes flickered, very green, behind her glasses, just for a moment, then she said, 'We've waited long enough. I'll leave Cassie a note.'

She picked up a used envelope from the littered desk, brought a pen from her pocket. I waited for her to begin writing on the back of the envelope, but she was standing quite still, staring at the square, forcefully-written address. I too had seen that writing somewhere...where? 'Harmony? What's wrong?'

'Hm? Oh, nothing. Nothing, I guess.' She put the envelope back, face down, precisely where she'd found it, tore a corner off a piece of wrapping paper, scribbled a few words and propped it on the bench.

We climbed back into the Datsun and continued along the loop road to join the main one. The car had been parked in the sun and was scorching inside. I rolled the windows right down to catch what air there was, air that smelled bracingly of salt, tar and fish. And another smell, so strong, rotten-egg and putrid that I choked and wound up the window again as fast as I could. '*What* was that?'

'I guess somebody ran over a skunk, squished him over the road. No use shutting the window, either. Could be there for a week or more. My dog once had a fight with a daddy skunk and we couldn't get near him for days. Guess what finally made him socially acceptable again?

Tomato juice. Can after can poured all over him. No kidding.'

I burst out laughing and wound the window down again, but though we must have travelled a further half mile I fancied I could still smell that ferocious scent.

A short while after coming out on to the main road we turned in between a pair of stone gateposts with a mailbox affixed to one of them. Stout chain-link fencing, six feet high, separated the property from its neighbours. The drive, long and straggly, turned to run through thick birch, oak and pine woods, roughly parallel with the coastline. Here and there large plantings of rhododendrons burst on us with a glory of bloom. Harmony drew the car up beside a small clearing. 'You get a wonderful view from up here. Worth getting out for.'

A pair of blue jays squawked indignantly and rose, flapping, jewel-blue against the dark pines as we stepped out and walked to the end of the clearing which sloped down to cliffs dropping sheer to the swell of the Atlantic. Standing on the top, we could see a succession of small bays and inlets that ran for miles before throwing out a long spit of rock terminated by a lighthouse. Along most of its length the coast looked fairly inaccessible, with woods running right to the cliff edge. Just to our left, far below us, was a tiny sheltered cove, a cuticle of silver-white sand lapped by a calm sea.

'That's where we bathe,' Harmony said, pointing down to it. 'You can get there by a path that leads down from the house. You can't see the house from here, the trees hide it.'

A solitary figure sat on the rocks, motionless, gazing out to sea, so still it was hardly possible to tell it was a human figure. Nearby was the carcass of a small boat, its ribs skeleton white, wedged in amongst the rocks, left for the sea to claim entirely.

It was so quiet. Nothing sounded in the still heat except the soft shushing of the sea below, but the rocks that hemmed in the wrecked boat were sharp and jagged, and a raft tossing on the waves further out in the bay marked the limits of safety, so that even within the shelter of the tiny beach reminders of danger were all about.

The figure on the beach stood up, waved to someone and began walking back along the shore. It was Max.

'Shall we go?' Harmony asked abruptly,

turning away, her voice flat.

In the clearing where the car stood waiting, the blue jays had come back and sat on a low branch, giving an occasional hoarse caw. Beautiful, brilliant creatures, unpleasant to think of them as the scavengers they were. They didn't fly away this time, and a small perky red squirrel eyed us as we approached, not moving either but making an indignant chattering at being disturbed. Then, thinking better of it, he turned and made off with jerky movements, to make an ineffectual scrabble at a pine tree any self-respecting squirrel would have shinned up in two seconds flat.

'Why, poor thing, he's lame!' Harmony cried softly, running up to him, but he dived into the undergrowth as she did so. 'Here, silly, I won't hurt you!' The animal, terrified, turned and lifted his lip, showing razor-sharp teeth.

'Watch it!' I warned. 'They bite.'

A sound of snapping twigs, someone passing, caused us both to turn round. There, at the cliff edge of the clearing, half turned from us to look out to sea, was a woman. My heart gave a great, dipping lurch. Hair lifting in the breeze, scarlet beach wrap blowing back to reveal a slim figure in a bikini, long legs, her arms extended to hold two dogs on a leash.

Not seeing us, she bent to unfasten the dogs, who immediately came loping back in our direction, and as she swung round to see why and faced us, the illusion shattered. It was simply that particular pose, the fact that her normally smooth hair was blowing free, her tall slimness, that had given Rowena that heart-stopping resemblance to the small gilded statuette of Lois.

The dogs came crashing on, two huge Alsatians—German shepherds they called them here—the size of small donkeys, one of them black as Satan.

'Rowena! Call them off, can't you?' Harmony shrieked. 'Oh, if you aren't the dumbest thing I ever saw, *now* you choose to come out!' This last to the cornered squirrel.

It was too late. The dogs, converging on us, had seen the creature. Harmony made a funny gurgling sound and closed her eyes. My hand went to my mouth. The squirrel screamed once, shrilly. Then it was silent. As the dogs fell on it, I rushed towards them, frantic, but

Harmony grabbed my arm and yanked me back. 'Don't be an idiot, they'll go for you.'

In any case, the dogs had already turned from the mess of torn flesh and bloody fur. They had probably eaten that day and were not hungry. They stood panting, weaving their enormous heads from side to side. The black one licked its chops and I turned away from the lolling tongue and great yellow teeth. I thought about being sick, looked at Harmony and decided one of us was enough. Rowena was standing several yards away.

'Oh no, oh no!' she was repeating, over and over. Then as suddenly as she had appeared she ran off, whistling to the dogs who obeyed immediately, leaping after her. The remains of the squirrel lay under the trees. The blue jays flew down into the clearing.

Harmony had her hand on the door handle. It was shaking.

'I'll drive,' I told her.

'No, I'm okay. Honestly. It's only a step away now, anyway.'

I pushed her gently to one side and got into the driving seat. We were both shaken and upset, but she more than I.

'Those damned dogs!' she said, white as paper as I started up and drove slowly along. 'They belonged to Lois, and Ewart Roscoe—he's Grandmother's handyman-caretaker—has to keep them locked up most of the time, but she won't hear of having them destroyed. They'll kill somebody one of these days. If they hadn't been with Rowena—' She broke off with a convulsive shudder.

'Oh, surely—'

'I'm not exaggerating.' She sat back and for the next few minutes we didn't speak, as we made our way slowly up the narrow drive. Then she leaned forward. 'Look, we're here.'

When she had declared how she hated the richness of Beacon Hill, indicating that Stonor's Point was more her style, I had assumed it to be a small—well, smallish—property, a rustic retreat, a New England homestead type possibly, where Stonors could relax from the cares of wealth and position and pretend to get back to the simple life.

It's never safe to assume anything.

Stonor's Point was big. By any standards. An irregular pile, rambling, turreted, a Brothers Grimm neo-Gothic edifice, it stood on the cliff top with its back to the sea, defiant of man and nature, strongly silhouetted against the empty sky, a flagged, railed terrace surrounding it like the deck of a ship.

Neglect would have supplied the creaking doors, the groaning shutters, the rusty iron keys that were all that was lacking, but after the first incredulous blink, I saw that it was immaculately well kept. The narrow drive opened out on to wide green lawns, smooth as a bowling green, bordered by thick shrubbery, circled with gravel. A spreading cedar stood in the middle of the central lawn, beds brilliant with annuals crept to the foot of the dark brick walls.

As I drew the car to a halt beside the house's front entrance, another was preparing to leave. Max, looking as if he belonged at Stonor's Point, as spruce and put together in sports shirt and casual slacks as in a formal business suit, was shaking hands with a big man in a loud check suit, pale and fattish, with prominent teeth like a rabbit. An unfortunate bow tie emphasised the resemblance.

'Thanks for calling,' Max said to him, as the man took his seat and started up,

'Keep me up to date.' Then to us, as the other car left, 'Leave the bags, I'll give you a hand later. You're just in time for tea. Isabella will be waiting.'

6

It was an unnerving experience. To step into a house I'd never before entered and recognise it as if I'd known it all my life.

The minute I walked over the threshold and into the huge and lovely galleried hall, I knew it. Its chestnut panelled walls, the painted, open-timbered roof, the glory of the great rich medieval-looking tapestry that glowed against the walls, the huge stone fireplace piled with driftwood, with blue Delft tiles set into its surround. Before I touched it, my fingers knew the silky feel of the patina on the long English oak refectory table, shipped over here at God knows what expense. The stained-glass lights in the windows of the fireplace alcoves, even the smell of the greenish euphorbia and syringa set out on the old inlaid grand piano in the corner seemed like things I had known all my life. My mother was very close to me.

I walked in a daze to where Isabella, sitting on a high-backed oak settle, its cushions covered in “greenery-yallery” William Morris cretonne, was presiding over a tea-table set with heavy silver and delicate china, and sat down opposite her in the oak chair she had indicated.

‘You would prefer coffee as usual, Harmony,’ she stated, pouring her a cup. ‘Cream? Strawberry shortcake? Tea for you Charlotte?’

Harmony took her coffee black and strong, gulping it down immediately, and I accepted a cup of tea gratefully. By unspoken agreement, neither of us mentioned the incident out in the grounds.

‘We’re not waiting for Rowena and Sebastian?’ Max asked, taking his cup from Isabella and drinking it standing up.

‘Rowena has gone for a swim,’ Isabella answered shortly, ‘and I don’t believe Sebastian will want *tea.* It’s a pity Colin couldn’t get here earlier,’ she added, picking up her own cup, ‘but he will be here in time for dinner.’

She avoided looking at Harmony as she threw this out with magnificent casualness. There was a moment’s utter silence. Harmony sat as if petrified, a piece of cake poised on her fork. ‘Colin?’ she repeated, dangerously quiet. ‘You’ve invited Colin?’

'Indeed. And why not, child?' A gentle smile played round Isabella's lips. Old as she was, I could have shaken her. That had been cruel.

Harmony put her fork down on her plate with a small clatter. '*Why not?*' she repeated. 'How can you ask? And he—accepted?'

'Naturally. This is a civilised society. He's been a guest for the last two years. It would have been ill-bred not to have included him this year, simply because of a small tiff.'

'Then I'm sorry. Ill-bred or not, you'll have to count me out.'

'Nonsense!'

'Grandmother, I mean it.'

'I'm afraid, dear, you have no choice.'

Throwing down her table napkin, Harmony jumped up, almost overturning the table, her calm abruptly deserting her. 'No? That's where you're so wrong! Just for once, you're not telling me what to do. I won't play your little games.'

'Come now, sit down, Harmony. Where is your self-control? You really cannot go through life avoiding every issue you find distasteful, you know.'

'Oh, but just you watch and see if I can't

avoid this one. Because I'm going to turn my car round this minute and head right back for Boston.'

Isabella's reasonableness left her at once. 'I think not. I think you will stay and behave yourself like a grown woman, not like a petulant child.'

Harmony glared back at her. The sun glinting through the stained glass on to her curly gold hair gave it a nimbus of light. Her eyes behind her ridiculous little spectacles looked very wide and very bright. With an eye on Isabella, Max, his own face set into an unreadable expression, reached out a hand and laid it warningly on Harmony's arm. She turned as if stung and gave him a reproachful stare, then flung his hand off and swung round on her heel. But instead of rushing outside to her car, she ran upstairs, the sound of her feet clattering on the polished boards as she ran round the gallery to the opposite side.

A door banged.

'When I was a girl,' Isabella observed, 'we learned to have more poise...though it isn't like her to be so rude. Well, I daresay she'll get over it.' She was a woman who found it very easy to convince herself, my grandmother, that things would be as she wanted them to be.

'All the same,' Max said, 'are you sure it's wise?'

'Wise?' Smiling, but imperious, she who must not be questioned.

'To have invited them both.' Meeting her look with some severity, he added dryly, 'You won't get them together that way, you know.'

'Did I say that was my intention?'

He raised an eybrow, but forbore to comment.

I wasn't altogether amazed that Isabella had invited Colin, but like Harmony I had to wonder why he'd accepted, knowing she would be here. To all intents and purposes he had conceded defeat where she was concerned. I tried to banish unworthy thoughts of his luxurious flat, and Harmony's considerable inheritance. There were undercurrents present, innuendoes I couldn't comprehend, shadows reaching from the past. I felt them stirring all around me in this house.

'They will have to meet some time,' Isabella was saying impatiently. 'A broken engagement doesn't have to mean a vendetta for life. Really, Max, it's quite ridiculous. Even divorced husbands and wives meet quite amicably these days. Or so I understand.' She lifted her cup, made a grimace of distaste when she found the tea was cold.

'Shall I get you another pot?'

'No, thank you, Charlotte, don't bother.' She sighed, leaned back in her chair, then changed her mind and began to get somewhat stiffly to her feet. 'I believe I'll go up now and take a short rest before dinner. I really am a little tired.' I had never before heard her admit to tiredness. One constantly had to remind oneself of her age, but at this moment she looked drained, emotionally and physically. 'Perhaps you'll show Charlotte to her room, Max? I've put her in the south turret room.'

He walked round and pulled out her chair for her, and we watched her cross the Bakshaesh rug and walk the length of the hall and up the stairs, a tiny upright figure, disdaining the assistance of the handrail.

'All set for a pleasant weekend,' I said when she'd disappeared. 'I hope Colin knows what he's in for.'

'Colin can take care of himself,' he said shortly, sitting down, and leaning back. 'But Harmony—maybe you can tell me what's going on? She hasn't flipped like that for years. Something's upset her—and I don't just mean her grandmother. She looked rattled when she came in. You too, I might say.'

'You're very observant.'

'I need to be. It's part of my job.'

'Well. There was an unpleasant happening as we got here.' I told him of the incident with the dogs. 'Are they really so dangerous? Harmony tells me Isabella won't hear of getting rid of them.'

'It's lonely out here, with no one but the Roscoes to look after the house and grounds most of the time. They're excellent guard dogs.'

'I'm sure! But would they really attack people?'

'Let's say I wouldn't advise petting them if you don't want your arm chewed off.'

I swallowed, picked up my cup and drank the rest of my now cold tea. It tasted horrible, but at least it was wet. 'I think I'd better get my things unpacked.'

Carrying both my cases, Max walked ahead of me up the stairs, turned right, and up another short flight set into the corner of the gallery. At the top was an arched door.

'Here we are,' he announced, pushing it open with his knee, then following me in. 'The turret room—one of the turret rooms. If you look out of the window, you'll see its twin on the opposite corner. Bathroom next door, and you'll have it all to yourself, by the way. All the other rooms on this floor are empty.'

The room was large, an unusual octagonal shape, full of its own nostalgic charm and character. Edwardian furniture, slender and ebonised, stood against wallpaper patterned with pale yellow leaf sprays; the carpet was gold and cream on a black background, with curtains in striped black and gold silk; two tub chairs were covered in velvet of the same glowing colour, and a Tiffany lamp stood by the bed.

It was, surprisingly, very cold.

I crossed to the deep bay window that bulged from one of the sides of the octagon to shut the wide-open window. Leaning out before I did so, I could see a terrace set with white chairs and tables directly underneath me, jutting to the cliff edge; the house seemed to be built as near to the brink as it could be without actually falling off, practically overhanging the beach on this side. The two bays were stuck on to the walls of each turret like blisters, with no corresponding projection beneath, so that standing in the window recess gave a curious impression of hanging in open space, with the sea below and the wide, uninterrupted spread of the sky above. I had a sensation of intense, sudden vertigo and I drew back, shivering in the breeze from the sea that stirred the curtains. Pulling at the open sash window to close it, I found it wouldn't budge.

'Here, let me. This room hasn't been used in years and those window cords might not be too safe.' Max came over and began to push the bottom section down.

If the room hadn't been used for years that perhaps explained the cold despite the heat of the day. But not why Isabella had put me here, alone on this upper floor. In this huge house, there must surely be other rooms available? 'This was my mother's room, wasn't it?' I asked Max.

'I believe it was,' he answered, giving me a quick look. 'The other was—was Ellen's. Nice rooms. I used to covet one of them when I came here for holidays with my brother when I was a kid, but they always put us on the other side of the house.' He smiled, and his eyes crinkled at the corners. 'I guess they thought it safer. You know what boys are.'

So Max had been a family friend, of the same social strata that would make him naturally acceptable as a husband for Lois. He had known them all since he was a child...

'Do you—do you remember my mother, Max?'

'Lydia? Why, surely. She wasn't a person you'd forget.'

'Tell me about her, please.'

'Well, I remember her, but I never *knew* her. I was just a kid and she was grown up and always so popular, you couldn't get near her for friends and admirers.' He added reminiscently, 'She always seemed to be laughing. I guess I was a bit dazzled by her...you must know what I mean. But after she went away to college, to take her degree, I never saw her again.'

No. I did not know what he meant. I sat down rather suddenly in one of the little velvet tub chairs. 'College?'

'Bryn Mawr, wasn't it—or Vassar, I'm not sure. She was always considered very bright.'

This was all news to me, all of it. Why had she never mentioned that she had a degree, never used her education, never taken up a career? She had devoted all her time and talents simply to being a wife...and a mother, of course.

And what about that other thing he'd said—what about *that?* 'Always laughing, surrounded by friends and admirers'? My *mother?* I was stunned.

She had had few friends, perhaps none who could truly qualify for that name. A quiet woman, sometimes even withdrawn. Except on rare occasions, the day of the kite-flying, for example. Yet it was because I could remember so clearly those few precious times that I found it suddenly not so strange after all to imagine her as Max remembered her.

What then had happened to change her?

He had perched himself on the edge of the small writing desk and I became aware that he was watching me rather closely.

'You never saw her again at all, after she went to college?'

He shook his head. 'As far as I was concerned, she just moved out of my orbit. You don't question these things when you're a child. I didn't know she'd run away until years later. I've never known why.'

'Haven't you ever wondered?'

'Maybe,' he shrugged. 'But since Isabella will never have Lydia's name mentioned—'

'What did she do that was so terrible, for heaven's sake?'

'That I don't know. I guess the only one who does is Isabella.'

Gripping the arms of my chair, I sprang up then walked over to the window, then turned to face the room, my back to the sea. 'I'm going to know, Max. I'm going to find out.'

He considered me, his eyes narrowed. 'I don't believe that would be too smart. Think again, Charlotte.'

'You believe it's better I should leave my mother as the skeleton in the family cupboard?'

'Has it occurred to you that what you might find could be worse?'

'I'm not afraid.'

'Carry on then, but you won't succeed,' he said quietly, but with a flash of warning in eyes once more grown hostile, that said *Not if I can help it* as plainly as if he'd spoken the words aloud.

'Maybe I won't, but that isn't going to prevent me from trying.'

'Is this some sort of crusade?'

'If you like.'

He came swiftly to stand by me, and with a force that frightened me gripped my wrist, looking steadily into my face. 'What makes you think you have the right to ferret out these old secrets? Leave them in the past, where they belong. Your mother is dead, but Isabella is still living. Isn't she entitled to her privacy?'

All my instincts screamed at the unfairness of that. Isabella was alive, yes, but her very silence was a slur on her daughter's name. If I didn't speak up for my mother, who would?

'My grandmother forfeited that right by asking me here, by demanding I take on family responsibilities. If she really wants me to become her heiress, well then she'll have to trust me, let me know the full story.'

He dropped my wrist like a hot coal, stuck his hands in his pockets and eyed me coldly. He said, very softly, 'Blackmail, Charlotte?'

A silence taut as a stretched elastic band twanged between us. 'I'm sorry, Max,' I told him defiantly, at last, 'but I'm going to do my damnedest to find out whatever I can.'

I lay on the bed for a long time after he'd gone, staring at the ceiling, then I unpacked my cases. The room, full of the glowing gold colour my mother had always loved, was saturated with her presence. I was half afraid to open the wardrobe in case I should find her dresses still hanging there, discover her silk underwear in the drawers like the heroine in some old novel, come across old letters in the desk.

Everything, however, was as bare and stripped as a hotel bedroom; fresh paper lined the drawers, the desk was empty. Not even the bookshelves gave a clue, for apart from one or two tattered favourites—*Little Women, Anne of Green Gables, Queechy*—only a few modern paperbacks and a pile of glossies rested there.

7

The character of Stonor's Point had everywhere been relentlessly preserved, even down to its plumbing—adequate but antiquated.

After I had unpacked, I took a bath in a large, high-ceilinged, chilly bathroom, with an old-fashioned bath as big as the QE2, pantomime-sized taps and a rubber ball and chain for a plug, so enormous it would have served to shackle the most desperate criminal. Nothing could have changed since my mother's day. It was of course one of the Stonor precepts that to show you had money enough to buy up the Rockefeller Foundation was vulgar; you didn't throw money around, you simply had it. And in any case, discomfort was redeemed by water that was scalding, and I'd been provided with a pile of huge, fluffy towels.

Overheated by my long soak, I found my room when I returned to it stuffy with its closed window. Cautiously, bearing in mind Max's warning about dodgy sash cords, I slid the window up from the bottom. Like something out of limbo, voices floated up from the terrace, and I heard my own name, clearly enunciated. I leaned perilously further out, interested to know who was down there discussing me, but the speakers were too far back on the terrace for me to be able to see them. The man's deep voice was one I didn't recognise; the other, lighter one could have been a woman's, but I wasn't sure. Odd words floated up to me, but nothing of which I could make any sense. Then the scrape of chairs, and silence.

We might be on vacation, but I suspected Isabella wouldn't look kindly on too-informal wear at the dinner-table, so I changed into a slim emerald green sheath, adding a glowing dark blue pendant. I was just slipping into my sandals when Harmony tapped on my door. 'May I come in, Charlotte?'

She too had changed. Her light Indian cotton dress with its full skirt gave her a slender femininity unguessed at in her usual garb, making her look at once older and paradoxically more vulnerable.

She came in, breathless with apologies. She was sorry for the scene at teatime, she ought to have had more control over herself, she had already apologised to Isabella, and been forgiven. 'But oh, Charlotte,' she said, perching on the edge of the delicate, turn-of-the-century ebonised dressing-table, fiddling with the things on it, absently helping herself to my precious 'Diorissima', 'you can't think how I'm dreading tonight. I'd every intention of going back to Boston, until Max came along and read me one of his lectures, and made me change my mind.'

'I can imagine.' She really did look apprehensive, and I thought she was hesitating over saying something else, but when she still didn't speak, I said, 'Never mind. Once the initial embarrassment's over, you probably won't feel so bad.'

'Embarrassment—is that what you call it? After not having had so much as a glimpse of Colin for a whole year? After what happened?'

I waited, expectant, and she bit her lip. Then she shrugged. 'Amongst other things, I told him I could never stand to look at him again,' she said, but I was sure that hadn't been all she'd meant to say.

'Well, he's hardly going to hold that against you for ever.'

Nervous as a kitten, she jumped up. 'Come on, let's get it over.' Then she added, sliding a wary glance at me and speaking carefully, 'It had to come, I guess, but I wish it had been anywhere else but here.'

'Does it make such a difference, being here?'

'Why yes. It was here, last year, when things went wrong, dreadfully wrong.' Nearly at the door, she paused. 'I guess it's one of the most awful things that can happen to a person, isn't it, when you find you've been let down by someone you trusted completely?'

I would need to have that explained, if she meant Colin, but mindful of my previous rebuff on the subject I knew I had to be careful how I went, and hesitating I was too late. As if regretting she had said as much as she had, she had already gone ahead of me, and though I hurried after her she was halfway down the short flight of steps to the gallery, with no chance of inviting further confidences.

As it turned out, she carried the occasion

off with a sang-froid worthy of my grandmother herself, and I was sorry Isabella wasn't there to see it, but pleading tiredness she had decided to take her meal in her room. It would have been difficult to guess at Harmony's trepidation. If her smile was just too brilliant, if she talked too much, it was behaviour everyone expected of her, and no one appeared to notice anything different about her. Except maybe Colin, who couldn't take his eyes off her, whose face tightened like a closed fist as he observed her coolness, her supposed indifference to their meeting.

Dinner that night was an informal affair, laid out as a buffet on the lighted terrace that overhung the beach. The bloom of the candles, the soft background music, the light delicious food, would have helped an awkward evening along if necessary, but it promised to pass agreeably enough. Everyone was on their best behaviour, maybe in deference to the pleasant elderly couple who had joined us, a Mr and Mrs Bruce, friends who were staying with their son nearby. Maybe the generous supply of wine helped, too. No doubt it was due in part to the absence of Isabella's inhibiting presence.

Sebastian, to do him credit, had completely taken over as host. He liked everything to be smooth and easy; perhaps he was too lazy to cope with anything more. He moved amongst us, keeping the ball rolling. He had rooted out an old gramophone and a pile of 78s to go with it. "Begin the Beguine" was scratchily turning when Edward Bruce came to take a seat beside me where I sat a little apart from the others.

'I'm glad to have the opportunity to talk with you, my dear. Lydia's girl, eh? Well, well.' He smiled charmingly, a tall old man with shrewd twinkling grey eyes. 'Not like her to look at, are you? You favour your grandmother, but I've been watching you, you don't lack Lydia's spirit. It was a sad shock to hear she'd passed on.' He shook his head. 'Seemed like she was still the little girl I'd dandled...I was her godfather, you know, as well as the family lawyer.'

As I listened to that deep, mellow voice, I knew it had been the one I had heard on the terrace earlier; I was equally certain that his companion had been Isabella, and that there was a distinct possibility that she and her lawyer had been disposing of my future—and if I had heard, who else?

However, that was of less importance at the moment than what he had said about my mother. 'You were her godfather? I didn't know. I never knew anything about her background.'

'She should have come back,' he said abruptly, 'if only for a visit, and brought you. I would have liked to have met your father, too. I wrote and asked her to consider it, years ago, but she refused.' He fell into an abstracted silence, while I waited impatiently for him to go on, eager for anything this kindly-disposed man could tell me.

I had to prompt him at last. 'You wrote to her? You knew where my mother was living?'

'Not at first. But I was the one who traced her, eventually. Not that it did much good—except to bring you here to us.'

'Don't think badly of her, please. It couldn't have been easy for her to stay away.' This at least was something of which I was inherently sure.

'How could I ever do that? Think badly of Lydia? My dear, I loved her.'

Tears sprang to my eyes. 'You're the

first person—' I choked. 'I'm sorry. Are you staying long in the district?'

'Oh, coming and going,' he answered, and told me he was leaving his son's house the next morning to return to Boston. 'May nags me to retire,' he remarked with a wry smile directed at his serenely plump wife, 'but we lawyers, we tend to die in harness.'

'Then please,' I begged urgently, 'if you're leaving, please tell me now. I so desperately need to talk to someone about my mother. What happened to make her leave? I'm sure you know.'

He made no attempt to deny it, but considered his reply in grave silence. At length he said, 'If I told you that the circumstances—as I know them—involved death, and shame, and grief, would you still want to know?'

'Yes,' I said in a low voice, after a moment.

'Charlotte, my dear!' A deeply troubled look was bent on me. 'I'd like to help you, believe me, but it wouldn't help, quite the reverse, take it from me. And in any case, you must realise my first duty is to your grandmother.'

As if rehearsed, right on cue, I became

aware of a distinct tension in the atmosphere. Swinging round on my seat, I saw Isabella standing in the doorway, every eye on her, her deep red robe falling in sculptured folds to the ground, adding apparent height and dignity to her small stature. A hush had fallen; only the singer sobbed on. "...what moments divine, what rapture serene..."

Her footsteps deliberately slow, she walked across to the record player and with a swift autocratic movement tore back the arm. The needle screeched protestingly across the surface, ruining the record for all time. In the silence, she turned to face us.

'Who,' she demanded, 'is responsible for removing the photographs?'

Her eyes fixed unwaveringly on Rowena, and Rowena, elegant and sophisticated in a long navy silk jersey dress which left one tanned shoulder bare, blushed and stammered like a gauche adolescent. 'I thought, Grandmother, I wanted—'

'Please see that they are put back. In their rightful places,' Isabella said, so gently I had to strain to hear her.

With the same unhurried deliberation, she turned and left the terrace. No one spoke or moved for several seconds. 'Sebastian?' Max prompted coldly.

Sebastian stood up, ignoring the hint. 'Don't you think we should all have another drink?'

Rowena was already on her way out by the time he'd finished speaking. I made a hurried excuse to Edward Bruce and followed her, through the dining-room and into the small front parlour still hallowed with the name of Grandfather Ralph's Study: a good-sized room, panelled like most of the other ground-floor rooms at Stonor's Point, a carpet square on the polished boards, an open fireplace, bookshelves round the walls, and dominated by a life-sized portrait in oils of Ralph, over the mantel.

I found Rowena kneeling in front of a low chest, carefully taking out a pile of framed photographs and placing them one by one beside her on the floor. Her pose as she knelt was curiously submissive, her bent head and her hair, dividing at the neck, giving her a defencelessness that was touching.

'May I help?'

She twisted round quickly, obviously so

intent she hadn't heard me come in, and shook her head. 'I can manage.'

'A bit unnecessary of Isabella, wasn't it?'

'No, no, it was my own fault. She'd every right to be angry. I shouldn't have taken them down without permission.'

'Fair enough. But even so, her lack of spirit irritated me she'd *no* right to make such a big production of it.'

I saw her stiffen, and feared I'd gone too far, but she only blinked and turned back to what she'd been doing. She raised no objection, however, when I bent to help her gather the frames together and pile them on to the large desk. There were upwards of thirty, many of them big enlargements, heavily framed, most of them apparently taken here at Stonor's Point, and all of them, inevitably, contained Lois.

'Shall I give you a hand to put them up?'

'Thank you, but I wasn't intending to do them now! I guess she'll just have to wait until Roscoe can put back all the hooks I had him take out.' Well, that was better, I thought, but fiddling with the string on the back of one of the frames, she added bleakly, so low I only just heard, 'I only wanted to help her.'

Her hands were trembling and I could only wonder, baffled, why she had made a gesture so pointless, guaranteed to put her out of Isabella's favour, when she so clearly longed for it. Isabella's reaction had been entirely predictable. Why must Rowena constantly batter her head against the brick wall of my grandmother's hostility? Sebastian's snide remarks about her liking for the martyr's role perhaps weren't all that far out.

She began stacking the frames together, the largest at the bottom. Even in stress, she couldn't resist twitching things into order. I handed them to her, until I came to a coloured snapshot of two little girls, bridesmaids at a wedding, holding nosegays, arms entwined. One smiled confidently into the lens. Lois, of course. And the other was Rowena, a thin little girl with an anxious gap-toothed grin, holding her head as if afraid her headdress of silver leaves might slip. 'You must have been of an age, you and Lois. You look like sisters.'

'We were raised like sisters by Grandmother. Lois was a year older than me.' I knew Rowena was thirty-three. She looked older, especially tonight. 'Richard divorced his first wife soon after Lois was born, and I hardly remember my own mother.'

'I didn't realise you'd been so close.'

'Close?' Her wry glance fell back to the snapshot. 'A lot of water has flown under the bridge since that was taken. You don't remain children for ever. We grew up, and apart. Even sisters aren't obliged to love one another,' she added with a curiously defensive look at me, brittle as eggshells. 'And Lois...well, she wasn't a very lovable person, except maybe to Grandmother.'

She went on stacking the frames neatly in order. 'This one is you, too, isn't it?' I handed the last one to her and she nodded. For once, Lois was a shadowy figure in the background. The small girl standing on the shore at the edge of the waves, a large shell held out on her palm, tense with concentration, could only be Rowena. A woman stood smiling down at her, her hand on the child's shoulder. Isabella, younger, but not greatly changed.

'You see, she didn't always hate me.' Rowena stared down at the photograph. 'She did her best to be fair. It's only since Lois died that she's turned against me. She believes I was to blame.'

She spoke without emotion, but something crossed her face as she spoke, something I wished I hadn't seen, immediately erased, but unforgettable. There was little doubt that Rowena had not only grown apart from Lois, she had come to detest her. Clearly, too, it was Rowena herself who couldn't bear to have the photographs of Lois around, no matter how she might rationalise her motives for removing them. There was so much anger in her that she wouldn't let out. I didn't like to think what might happen if ever she did.

'Of course, she's right, in a way,' she went on, still in that controlled voice, turning her anger in on herself. 'It was my fault. We'd had a terrible quarrel that day. I should never have provoked her—she always did something reckless after any upset, as if she could get it out of her system that way.' Her voice broke suddenly and tears began to pour down her cheeks. She rubbed them away with the back of her hand, like a child.

I put my arms round her. She felt light as a bird, her bones brittle and thin. The scent she wore was hesitant and elusive, very like Rowena herself. 'Don't be kind to me!' she cried, springing away. 'Not you, above all.'

'What?' I cried, taken aback. 'What have I done?'

'Oh, it isn't anything you've done.' She turned away. I understood the recoil had been involuntary, and though it cost me dear, I held back from pressing her to explain. She was very near the end of her tether. I followed her as she walked listlessly to the door.

Strains of music could still be heard coming from the terrace. 'I'm going right to my room. I can't face any more of that,' she said, pressing the light switch of the study, closing the door behind us and half turning at the foot of the stairs. Soft lamplight suffused with radiance the great glowing hunting tapestry on the wall behind her, cruelly lit her tense, tear-stained face, and when she spoke it was with difficulty. 'I—I'm sorry, I don't seem to have any control of myself these days. But thanks—for the moral support. It was thoughtful of you. I won't forget that, Charlotte.'

The terrace when I returned to it was empty, except for Sebastian, lying back in a chair, his feet on the rail, the inevitable glass in his hand. His profile, outlined against the lamp, looked dark and enigmatic; even, for a flickering moment, frightening. He turned and saw me and his teeth gleamed. 'Ah, the good little Samaritan!'

I said shortly, 'Rowena was obviously very upset.'

'She's better left on her own when that mood takes her,' he said, bland as porridge. 'She gets hysterical and says things she doesn't mean.' I said nothing. 'She has a vivid imagination,' he prompted, but I wasn't going to be pushed into telling him what had passed between Rowena and myself. He waved his glass towards the seat beside him. 'Come and sit down. Everyone suddenly had urgent business elsewhere as soon as the Bruces left. Harmony's gone to bed, Colin for a walk, I ask you! I don't know where Max is. Won't you save me from utter desolation and join me in a nightcap, cousin Charlotte?'

I wanted nothing less. I could do without Sebastian any time, tonight more than somewhat.

'Oh, there you are.' It was Mary McDermott, anxiously peering round the door, looking for me. 'Your grandmother's compliments, and will you step up to her room for a few minutes?'

I hesitated only fractionally. Faced with the choice, an encounter with Isabella was only a little more enticing than a tête-à-tête with Sebastian, but I didn't see how I could refuse. 'Sebastian, if you'll excuse me? I'll say goodnight.'

He inclined his head, spreading his hands philosophically, his sardonic, saurian smile gleaming out again. 'Goodnight. Sleep well.'

'Come in Charlotte,' Isabella said, 'and sit down. But first, if you would be so good as to bring me that box from my bureau, and my purse beside it.'

I came into the still, hot, orchid-perfumed room, collected the handbag and the carved cedarwood box, put them on to the walnut table next to her chair, and took a seat beside her as she indicated. 'One has to be so very careful,' she remarked, selecting a small key from a bunch she extracted from her bag, and fitting it into the lock of the box. It gave a tiny click, and she changed the key for another which completed the unlocking. 'And even so, something was stolen from me last year.' Her glance slid sideways, yet alert for my reaction.

'Stolen? Something valuable?'

'A sapphire and diamond necklace, French, part of a set,' she said, sitting very upright. 'Worth a great deal in terms of money, but I happen to be fond of it, which upset me far more.'

'Weren't the police able to catch the thief?'

'The police, Charlotte, were not brought into it. Since—I might as well be frank—since it was taken from me by one of my own family.'

'What?' If she had wanted to shock me, she had now succeeded.

'Oh, yes.' Her fingers beat a small tattoo on the arm of her chair; the lamplight drew fire from her rings. 'I wasn't, naturally, prepared to make a scandal of it. Besides, they would have needed proof, and I had none, none that they would regard as such. Myself, I was quite convinced.' She paused, toying with the little key. 'I had Lois's word, you see. She told me who was responsible.'

I watched a moth dancing round the lamp in ever-decreasing circles, a beautiful, delicate, furry creature, seeking its own death. 'You knew who took it—and you haven't got it back?'

Her chin lifted, proud, autocratic. 'Do you imagine I would *ask* her? I believe she thinks I haven't missed it. It was a piece I had not worn in years...in fact, it was only by a misunderstanding that it had been brought with one or two other things from the bank where it was kept.'

'Her, you said, you wouldn't ask *her*?'

The cold in her eyes deepened. 'Oh let's not mince words. It was Rowena who stole it, who else.'

I privately thought it might have been almost anyone else except Rowena. I said, 'I must say I find that a fairly incredible thing to believe.'

'Do you think I found it easy?'

Rowena, believing Isabella's bitter feelings stemmed from what she imagined was her part in Lois's death. 'Are you saying,' I asked slowly, 'she doesn't even know you suspect her?'

There was evasion in the way she began to fumble amongst the contents of the box, she who was always so decisive, so precise in her actions, but she wouldn't be shaken. She gave a tight little smile. 'If she can live with her conscience, I can live with the knowledge of what she has done to me.'

'Not even allowing her to speak in her own defence?' I could scarcely credit this.

'What defence has she? The necklace is gone. Oh, I don't think she took it for herself, she's not that type...I doubt she would have the courage, for one thing,' she said, dryly sarcastic. 'It was for that husband of hers...she's besotted enough to do anything for him.'

In this Isabella was behind the times, I thought. I opened my mouth to protest at the unfairness of judging anyone unheard, but when I looked at her closed face I knew I should be wasting my time. The subject as far as she was concerned was closed, and she was already taking out one of several chamois leather bags from the box, loosening the ribbon with which it was tied, carefully selecting from its contents and handing something to me. 'Try this on, Charlotte. It's a family heirloom I should like you to have.'

I drew back. 'No. You mustn't give me things.'

'I *want* you to have it,' she stated, her customary response to any opposition, holding out her hand. On her palm glowed a great antique ring, a deep red carnelian set in heavily worked gold. I hated it immediately, violently; it was cumbersome and ugly. My hands would be much too small and blunt-fingered to carry it off. I took it and thrust it on my finger to demonstrate its total unsuitability. 'There.' I spread my hands to show Isabella, then pulled it off again. 'It doesn't fit, it's much too big.'

'Nonsense.' Grasping my hand, refusing to admit defeat, she slid the ring on to my middle finger. 'What's wrong with that? It can't fall off now.'

'Maybe not, but it still slips round, and that's uncomfortable. In any case, I won't—'

A tap on the door interrupted my protest and it was opened in answer to Isabella's command to enter.

'Oh, sorry, I didn't know you had company,' Max said to Isabella. 'I only popped in to see if you were settled for the night.' He made to withdraw. As he did so, his eyes went to the jewel box, then to my hand, where the ring glowed like a great gout of blood.

'Don't go, I was just leaving.' Pulling the ring off once more, I thrust it back at Isabella. 'I'm sorry,' I said to her.

'I'll have it made smaller.' she replied, imperturbably disregarding any feelings I might have, the taut anger that must have shown on my face. 'Charlotte and I have just finished our business, Max,' she went on, imperiously terminating further argument, 'and since there is nothing further I need tonight, I'll bid you both goodnight.'

Dismissed as from the presence of royalty, we left. The same thought must have occurred to him, too. I saw the amused twitch of his lips and laughed angrily as we began to walk along the gallery. 'It wasn't as you thought, in there. I've no intention of letting her bribe me with jewellery—or anything else.'

He stopped to put his hand on my shoulder, a gesture his patients must find reassuring and calming. One almost caught the whiff of antiseptic. 'How you let things rankle! Isn't a man allowed one mistake?' He stood looking down at me. 'You need some fresh air to cool off,' he said suddenly. 'Let's take a turn on the beach, where we can talk.'

'My turn for a lecture?'

For a moment he looked puzzled, then

gave a short laugh. 'I see Harmony's been talking. No, strictly none, I promise. Fetch your coat, it's chilly down by the shore. And don't forget to change those bits of nonsense.' He glanced at the four green straps and two slender heels that called themselves a pair of sandals, and smiled again.

'I amuse you?'

'I was thinking, you put me in mind of an angry dragonfly,' he said, touching the green silk of my sleeve, 'with those flashing blue eyes and that fierce little face. You're not scared of anything, are you, Charlotte?'

So even Max Remmick could be wrong at times.

Despite my light coat, I noticed the chill as we stepped from the house into the coolness of the evening, drawing in deep breaths of fresh scented air compounded of pine resin, night-scented plants and the salt sea smell.

We followed a path through the woods, one which wound narrow and stony through the trees, ending up on the beach beside a tumbledown, weathered wooden beach hut. He went in front of me, turning as we came to the last few feet to give me a hand, keeping hold of mine as we walked along the silver-gold sand, firmed by the receding tide. When we came to a flat outcrop of rocks we sat, watching the sea. I wondered whether he would say anything about the scene Isabella had created on the terrace, what he thought about it. I would have liked, too, to hear him confirm my own feeling that it was impossible to think of Rowena having stolen the necklace, but since both subjects were so intimately bound up with Lois I felt hesitant about broaching them myself and he didn't attempt to, either.

We talked spasmodically, perched on the flat stones, listening to the shush of the waves on the shore, the occasional call of an owl from the woods behind, but the intervening silences weren't unfriendly, and I felt for the first time we were at ease with one another. He spoke a little about his boat which he was planning to pick up from its winter moorings down the coast, and of the holidays he'd spent here, ever since he was a child.

'It's always been like a second home. I'd forgotten how good it is to be here,' he remarked, 'just being able to relax, leave everything behind.'

'Still, you love your job—you really care about being a doctor. It isn't just something you do for a living.'

'Of course.' A pause. 'Don't you feel that way about teaching?'

'Not really, not like my father did. I haven't his patience, for one thing, nor his gift with children. I couldn't be as good as he was, not in a million years.' Remembering him, I warmed as I spoke. Max made no answer...and I saw myself as he must see me, glowing with adolescent father-worship. Aghast at this unexpected glimpse of myself, I came back with a touch of bravado, 'I'm not totally irredeemable, though. I do love the subject I teach, history.'

'Then why not use it in a job you really like?'

I met a man once who had a theory about teachers. Their trouble was, he said, they never left school, college being an extension of their schooldays, teaching a return to them. They never had a chance to reach maturity. I had laughed and been half-shocked by his cynicism. Yet here I was, twenty-seven and still afraid to step from behind my father's shadow, to take the plunge and do...what I'd wanted to do for so long. Well, why not? Why all the uncharacteristic caution over this? Because this mattered so much, because I was afraid of failure?

'You're not married,' Max said suddenly. 'There's some man, back home?'

I thought about Graham. 'No.'

'You surprise me.'

If the remark was meant to flatter, the dry tone was not, and I believed I understood very well what he meant. More than one male scalp hung at my belt, affairs that had come to nothing, because that was how I wanted it. No strings. 'Nothing permanent,' I said.

'Against marriage on principle, or for more personal reasons?'

'Am I against it? Well, maybe. Some of us are.'

'Why?'

'Possibly because it seems such a selfish thing. There's no room for anyone else.'

The locked bedroom door. The way they sat close together on the sofa, so that as a small child I would wriggle myself between them. The hurt when they always kissed each other first, before me. Not that either my father or my mother had meant to exclude me. There wasn't any doubt that they had both loved me dearly. Only they had loved each other more.

That was something I had been forced to accept, but I buried it deep, and now I never thought about it. We all have problems of one sort or another, growing up.

Max Remmick was too perceptive by half, however, watching me with that clinically observant look, seeing what I had half-forgotten. But never forgiven, Charlotte, never truly forgiven. Slowly, I felt something easing inside me. The finger that had pressed for so long on the secret flaw at the heart of me had lifted.

He still didn't take his eyes off me, and the silence lengthened. Became charged, until my heart started to beat slow and thick, hammering against my ribs. I stood up, and in the same moment he was standing beside me. 'Do you want to go on, Charlotte?' There was nothing in his face to tell me his thoughts, but I nodded. Breathless. Feeling I was in some way committing myself to something destined to bring me nothing but trouble, and not caring.

A shadow fell between us. Mysterious, unsummoned.

Abruptly, he set off walking again, holding my hand, heading towards the point where the ribs of the skeleton boat stood starkly white, gripped between the big grey rocks. Cruel enough from above, from here, exposed by the tide, they looked like a double row of fangs. Instinctively, I slowed.

Max showed no such hesitation, keeping a firm pressure on my hand so that I was forced to quicken my pace. At last he said, his profile unsmiling, 'It's only a place, some dangerous rocks. Lois died there, sure...which is no reason for investing it with superstitious significance. That's a lot of wasted emotion, and it's the way horror stories grow.'

I think I had known it must have been there that she died, ever since I had looked down from the cliff top earlier and seen him sitting there, motionless, beside the wreck. 'That's dreadful,' I said softly. But so rational. So dispassionate. There was no answer to it, and the quality of my silence gave me away.

He swung me round, his face anything but dispassionate. 'You think it better if I wear my heart on my sleeve?'

The moon shone full on him, stripping away the image he chose to show to the world, and seeing the ravaged face beneath I felt a rush of strange emotion, a plunging, unreasoning twist of panic, an inexplicable premonition so strong it was like a knife turning in me. Yet, even as fear raced through my mind, the mask was resumed; he was once more the strong, controlled, responsible doctor. He would never make concessions to himself, any more than to others. Was that what had frightened me so much about him?

I had no means of telling, but one thing I did know now. That shadow that had fallen between us was Lois.

'I didn't mean that to sound as I did,' I said, ashamed of a facile judgement that had so easily condemned him as unfeeling. I too had walked in the dark, after my father's death. 'We seem to have a capacity for misjudging one another, don't we? I spoke without thinking, a thing I'm rather apt to do.'

'I had noticed.' He smiled, but I wasn't sure he liked my apology. He didn't apologise much, himself. 'Other things as well, though, nicer things. Like going after

Rowena tonight when Sebastian should have gone.'

'Oh. Oh, well, Sebastian's pathetic.'

He gave me a quick, sharp glance. 'If you believe that to expect more out of life than you're prepared to put into it is pathetic, yes, he is.'

Life as an equation. Yes, I agreed with that. But I thought Max was in fact trying to tell me something else, because he wasn't one for philosophising much, either.

8

I set my travelling clock on the table beside my bed, feeling the events of the day wound up in me as tightly as the spring inside it. I didn't expect sleep to come easily, but gradually, gazing out at the star-pricked sky, lulled by the murmur of the sea below, my over-stimulated senses quietened and I slid into a quiet, deep sleep.

What woke me in the small hours I don't know. I stirred and then was fully awake, alerted by something which penetrated my sleeping consciousness. All was silent. I lay awake, straining my ears, but I could hear nothing except the odd creak which all old houses give during the night, as if they too stir and settle sometimes in their sleep.

The water pipes in my room gave a noisy gurgle. I hadn't been aware that the plumbing on the floor below could so easily be heard up here; it wasn't noticeable, certainly, during the day. Fully awake now, and thirsty, perhaps through an association of ideas, I slipped out of bed and pulled my dressing-gown on to fetch a drink of water from the adjoining bathroom.

As I stepped outside my door, a figure slid softly towards me, its white garment floating, gliding noiselessly above the carpet. Fright jerked at me. If it hadn't at that very moment penetrated my half awake state that I had heard, a second before I saw that figure, a door being pulled to along this corridor of unused rooms, I might well have thought it was one of the Stonor ghosts.

At first I thought Rowena was sleep-walking, then I saw she had seen me, silhouetted in the lamplight from the room behind me. She stopped, and I felt for the switch on the wall. Dazzled in the sudden illumination, she shaded her eyes. 'I'm sorry if I woke you—I thought I smelled smoke,' she said quickly, nervously.

'Smoke?' I sniffed, fancying I did indeed smell a faint acrid odour. 'We'd better take a look around then, hadn't we?'

'No, no,' she intervened hastily. 'I've already searched thoroughly. I made sure everything's safe.' I watched her push her hair back with those long white fingers and thrust them into the pockets of her light cotton robe.

'Well then...if you're sure...'

We said goodnight. I waited until she reached the bottom of the stairs, then I went back into my room, shutting the door firmly behind me. I let ten minutes go by, then as quietly as I could opened my door again and crept along the corridor.

The door from which Rowena had come wasn't a very good fit and hadn't closed properly behind her. I pushed it wide open, switched the light on and stood on the threshold, looking in. And a feeling of trespass came over me, which was silly, because Isabella had urged me to explore the house, telling me I was free to go wherever I wished. Shaking off the feeling, I stepped inside.

It was evident that the room had been occupied more recently than by Rowena's mother. The decorations, the furniture, were ultra-modern, entirely unlike any other room at Stonor's Point, where tradition prevailed and possessions gathered by generations of Stonors remained as sacrosanct as their money. I stood in the middle, looking around, trying to capture a recent tantalising memory.

Max had told me yesterday to whom this room had belonged—once. Before he'd said 'Ellen' however, he had hesitated, and I knew now he had just stopped himself from saying 'Lois'. I felt I had come to know her well enough by now to appreciate that the dashing scarlet and beige colour scheme could only be hers. A sophisticated, neo-Art Deco room much given to cream leather, chrome and glass, with Bauhaus style chairs and shiny veneered panelling behind the bed.

In one corner of the room was a small washbasin. It was clean, but still damp. I finally found what I was looking for on the buff carpet beneath; minute charred flakes of the paper which had been burnt there, which had left the tell-tale traces I had noticed on Rowena's fingers, and the odour clinging to her robe.

The beach wore a very different aspect the next morning before breakfast. The sun was hot already, and the water placid in the little bay. Running in until I was out of my depth, I began swimming out to the small raft that marked the danger point.

Despite the heat of the sun, the temperature of the buoyant water took my breath away. I swam strongly at first, enjoying the powerful feeling of cutting cleanly through the waves, the coldness tingling against my skin, but when I reached the raft and pulled myself on to it, I knew I'd reached my limits. Breathless and exhilarated, I squeezed the water from my hair and sat with knees hunched, dripping, glowing from the exercise, the sun hot on my back.

If last night was an example of what the next few days at Stonor's Point were going to be, I thought, spreading myself to the sun, I could view the prospect without enthusiasm. There was an unhappy atmosphere lying over the place, not entirely due to Isabella stirring things up. Too much was unexplained. Including Max's attitudes. Heat flooded my body as self-knowledge returned in the memory of that moment on the beach.

I heard a splashing behind me and rolled over, raising my head to see Colin, recognisable by his bobbing red head, swimming in from the shore. 'You're an early riser!' he called, reaching out a hand.

'Too lovely a morning to loll in bed.'

Hauling himself on to the raft, he shook

himself like a dog. 'Saw you from the beach and it seemed like a good idea. Not intruding, am I?'

'Of course not. Welcome on board.'

'Start as you mean to go on,' he said, settling himself beside me. 'Getting this time off, Max and myself together—it's taken so much organising, I'm not going to waste any of it. Swim before breakfast, reading, a walk before lunch. Might even get in some golf.'

'That sounds like a lot more organisation!'

'Och, well. It's something of a working weekend, anyway. Max wants to rough out an idea for a project he has in mind.'

'I'm sure he'll let you off the reins occasionally.'

'I'm not asking any favours,' he came back quickly, touchily, without humour. 'It's my due.' Unwilling to admit that by coming here he was out to do himself a bit of good in Max's eyes. He added, veering round the subject in a lumbering way, 'You're going to take it easy, too?'

'No fear. I'm going to be made to work, as well.'

'Good Lord.' He rolled himself over on to his stomach, propped himself up on his elbows, and stared at me.

I laughed. 'I'm doing it because I want to, as well. Those family papers I told you about. Isabella thinks that written up they'd make an interesting book.' For the first time, it occurred to me to wonder if she had, with that uncanny intuition she sometimes showed, guessed about me. About my own aspirations.

'Hm.' Colin leaned over the edge of the raft, cupped water in his hands and let it fall in sparkling, chandelier drops. I hadn't been alone with him since that evening I had burst in on him at his flat, and I braced myself against the demand for an explanation I felt coming. But all he said was, 'Don't let her overwhelm you, Charlotte.'

'I won't.'

'They all say that, but in the end they all do her bidding. However much they resent it.'

Somewhere above the bay, from the gardens, came the sound of a motor mower. All around the house, the smooth lawns and shrubberies lay serene and smiling. The sea smacked gently at the edges of the raft. The sky was like mother of pearl. I thought about

Rowena, here in spite of all her talk of refusing. Of how I myself might well have been manoeuvred, of Harmony, staying yesterday. I remembered what she had said about Colin...and something else.

'Have you managed to get your shoes cleaned up?' His eyebrows jerked up in surprise. 'I met Mary with them at arm's length as I was coming out,' I explained.

'Oh, that! I went for a walk last night, and trod where a skunk had been before me. It's a gey powerful odour, is it not? Apparently, Mary has an infallible recipe for getting rid of it.'

'Tomato juice.'

He laughed but remembering where I'd encountered that smell before, I didn't altogether share his amusement. 'I'm getting chilly. I'm going to swim again,' I said.

He put a square, freckled hand out and I sat up. 'They've warned you not to go near the rocks over there?'

I followed the direction of his pointing finger to the sharp spit of rocks where the wreck was wedged. The chain-link fencing that marked the boundary either side of this private beach had been brought right down to the water's edge, the supports driven into the rock. He added quietly, ‘That’s where she drowned.’

‘I’ve been told, but not how it happened. That boat—?’

‘No, no, that’s been there for years. She went for a midnight bathe, dived and hit her head on a rock. It was a game she used to play, a sort of Russian roulette, though she claimed she knew exactly the right spot to dive, into a channel between the rocks.’

‘Only this time she miscalculated?’

‘The tide was going out; there wasn’t enough water. By the time she was found, it was too late. It was the dogs who gave the alarm. They howled like banshees until Max went down.’

‘She took the dogs with her when she went swimming?’

‘They went everywhere with her. She used to whistle and they’d come running to join her.’

I closed my eyes, imagining the shock that must have gripped them all...Max, going down to the beach, finding her drowned, beautiful body mangled on the rocks. Rowena, desperate with remorse because she believed their quarrel must have precipitated Lois’s action. Isabella, so little able to reconcile herself to the facts she could only explain it as an act of violence against Lois, the ultimate violence, murder.

Murder by whom? Sebastian had said that everyone staying in the house had reason to be glad she was out of the way. Why? Why had they all been on such bad terms with Lois?

'What was she like—as a person?' I asked Colin. 'I know she was beautiful to look at—how did she get on with other people?'

He didn't answer for so long, I began to think he wasn't going to, but he was merely thinking out his reply in his usual thorough way. 'She was—exciting,' he said at last. 'Fun, when she wanted to be, full of spunk and courage. But selfish, egotistical, mean as hell if she didn't get her own way. Spoiled rotten by Isabella. People quite often detested her.'

'Enough to want to kill her?'

He sat up and looked narrowly at me. 'Now where'd you get those sort of ideas?'

'Nobody's made a secret of it. Isabella thought someone did. Rowena said she made a public accusation.'

'I was there when she said that. "It amounts to murder" was what she said, and that's quite different.'

I was shocked by the way he looked as he spoke. His eyes were sea-green, cold. His face looked white and set under his red hair. He saw me staring at him, and gave a self-conscious laugh. 'Poor Charlotte, you've stumbled into a sticky situation, haven't you?'

'I wouldn't mind so much if I knew what it was all about.'

'You're better off not knowing. Confine your researches to those dead and gone Stonors. The history of those still living isn't nearly so pretty.'

I was beginning to think I was more than willing to do this. I was becoming ever so slightly fed up with the subject of Lois. She had been a not very nice individual, it seemed to me—and yet one whose personality reached out from beyond the grave to touch all those with whom she'd been in contact. But I had never known her, and she was dead, and her death was nothing to do with me. I had other purposes in coming here than endlessly discussing Lois Remmick.

'You *are* cold, Charlotte,' Colin said suddenly, 'You're goose-pimpled. Race you to the beach.'

He beat me, easily. I only just made it. I didn't think I'd attempt that raft again.

'I'm somewhat afraid,' Isabella said, 'my husband wasn't a very practical—or a very tidy—man. He always *intended* to put these papers in order...'

I followed her across the sun-splashed carpet to the desk where several bulging boxes of papers had already been laid out. 'They've never been touched apart from the time Lois began...her patience gave out before she got very far.'

'I've plenty of time.' My mind was already working on how I would classify and sort into date and subject order.

Isabella paused with her hand on the doorknob. 'Don't waste too much of this lovely weather indoors. You're here on holiday, don't forget.' There was an unaccustomed kindness in her. She and I had ceased our sparring from the moment I had agreed to come to Stonor's Point; she could afford to be agreeable, to cloak that domineering streak in her personality, now that things were apparently going as she had planned. I would have felt more comfortable had I not been certain of the battle that awaited me when she learned

I had no intention of succumbing to her final purposes. So I trod carefully. She wasn't to be dealt with lightly, as I had already seen on various occasions, and to antagonise her was no part of my own purpose.

When she had gone, I settled down happily to arrange the papers, a cup of coffee at my elbow, the sun streaming through the small alcove window on my right. The desk stood beneath the open front window. Beyond it, on the main lawn, the great cedar spread its graceful branches.

I worked steadily through the boxes. Every letter ever received, copies of others sent out, every receipted bill for over forty years made for a sizeable pile. Within a very short space of time, the desk, most of the floor and every other available surface was covered with stacks of documents in some rough approximation of order. Three hours later, I was sitting back on my heels on the floor, admitting disappointment to myself. I had been so sure I must find some reference, however small, to my mother's past, but so far I had found nothing at all.

I was still kneeling there when Harmony

popped her head round the door. 'Grandmother's sent me to tell you lunch will be in a few minutes.'

'Lunch, already? Oh, I'm not hungry. I'll skip it.'

'She thought you might say that and told me to bring you along by force if necessary.' She grinned, and added, 'Self interest—she doesn't want you dying on the job.'

'Oh, all right.'

'How's it going?'

'He,' I said, pointing my ballpoint at Grandfather Stonor's portrait, 'was an old humbug.' He looked impassively down on us, a dark, melancholy-looking man, in his fifties when this portrait had been painted, shortly before he died. A fiddle-shaped face, down-drooping mouth, even his eyes having a sad downward slant. 'Letting everybody believe him such an efficient business tycoon. He probably lifted a finger and somebody else did it all for him. He must have driven his secretary mad.' I showed her what I meant.

He had had an infuriating habit of beginning letters, or scribbling memos to himself in his nearly indecipherable, cramped handwriting, on any old piece of paper that came to hand—the bottom of a bill would do, the back of a snapshot, someone else's letter—and the same jotting might well be continued on some other random scrap. Sometimes he had even made diary-like observations and records of family happenings in the same way, as if to imprint them on his mind. These were the sort of details which interested me most. The rest was pretty dull stuff, but all of it must be pieced together—no small task, since nothing was dated, nothing in sequence.

'You look as though you could use some help,' Harmony suggested, taking stock. 'Will I do?'

'Thanks, but I'm not sure. It's really a one-person job.' I didn't want to miss anything...nor did I want to have to admit that I was looking for anything specific. So far the only pertinent snippet from my point of view had been a yellowed newspaper clipping, an obituary notice for a Captain George Allot, killed in action in Korea, decorated with a Purple Heart for bravery. A dim photograph accompanied it, of a smiling young man in Army uniform, his cap at a jaunty angle. 'Captain Allot leaves a widow and five year old daughter,' the notice continued, going on to remind readers that the Stonor-Allot wedding, six years ago, would be remembered as one of Boston's weddings of the year, that Captain Allot's widow, Ellen, was the elder daughter of Mr and Mrs Ralph Stonor, of Beacon Hill. The five year old daughter of course would be Rowena.

I wished after all I had declined lunch. Afterwards, I felt reluctant to continue what I'd begun this morning; the dusty papers, yielding so little, had lost their promise. How gullible I had been to believe Isabella careless enough to leave lying around any written evidence of what she was so determined to conceal from me, I thought, disheartened, leaning on the terrace rail. The waters of the bay glittered, and a sailing boat rounded the point. Temptation lay outside in the guise of gardens yet to be explored, in coins of sunlight dappling the lawns beneath the trees. I gave in. I would find a quiet spot in the garden and look over the notes I'd made.

Returning to the study to fetch them, expecting to find it empty, I walked right in on a conversation between Max and the stranger he'd been seeing off when we arrived, the White Rabbit and the loud check suit. They were talking about Sebastian Garth when I came in. Max swung round with a quick movement. 'You had me jumping half out of my skin there, you came in so quietly,' he said.

'Sorry, I didn't know anyone was here. I just wanted some notes I left on the desk.'

'Don't let us interrupt your work. We were going anyway, we've almost finished.' He introduced his visitor as 'my friend Bernie Fisher.'

'Glad to make your acquaintance,' said Mr Fisher, his prominent front teeth very much in evidence. He was younger than I had at first thought. His eyes were a very clear blue, and sharp as needles.

'Like Sebastian, Mr Fisher is interested in old silver—he's an expert, and what he doesn't know about it isn't worth knowing,' Max said, and Mr Fisher smiled deprecatingly.

There was no cause for mistrust, no reason for supposing Max's oblique explanation for the other man's presence just a little too pat. Nothing to suggest that a client of Sebastian's could not be a friend of Max's at the same time. Stranger affinities existed. Nor, even if his sartorial tastes did run to cheap bright suits, did it mean that Mr Fisher couldn't also be a connoisseur of fine silver. So why did a warning bell jangle insistently at the back of my mind?

I found the gardens so much more extensive than I had supposed that, wandering around, I lost my bearings. Rounding a corner I came unexpectedly upon a weather-beaten little man wearing a deep-vizored bird's-beak cap and green overalls like a petrol-pump attendant, bending over a planting of white violas and heliotrope. This must be Roscoe, husband of the plump, capable woman who managed the house. I stopped to admire the flower beds and to introduce myself. 'You've a beautiful garden here,' I told him.

He looked pleased. 'Coming from an Englishwoman, that sure is a compliment. Stationed in England during the war, near York,' he said. 'Never forgotten your English gardens.'

'Near York? That's in my home county.'

He was interested to know whether the

city had changed, if the camp where he'd served still existed. I couldn't tell him that, but we talked about the Minster restoration and then, as he began his hoeing again, I asked if there wasn't another path down to the beach, rather than having to retrace my steps across to the one through the woods.

'Never been one,' he answered. 'Rocks go down too steep. A person can't even climb them from the bottom.'

'Oh well, I'll just have to go back, then. 'Bye for now.'

'You come along and see my orchid house, any time you've a minute to spare, Miss Haigh. Be glad to show you around.'

I left him, whistling, busy with his hoe, and walked around to the path, skirting the house and cutting into the edge of the woods. It was cool under the trees, and I enjoyed the springy feel of the beechmast beneath my feet, the tang of the sea-laden air. Negotiating the path, I came out just above the beach house that was tucked into the lee of the cliffs. I could see that a ramp led down from it to the sand, and supposed that might be where Max kept his boat. I was almost level with the window when I heard the voices.

'...changed your mind?' came the unmistakable voice of Cassie Hayter.

'No,' returned Colin Macintosh's Scottish tones, deep with emotion. 'No, I promise I'll never change my mind about you, Cassie.'

She laughed throatily.

9

I fled. Back up the precipitous path as if catapulted, looking out for Harmony so that I could prevent her going, by some ill chance, down to the beach. Then I remembered she had gone to play tennis with the younger Bruces at their home further up the coast.

Once back in my room, I sank on to the dressing-stool, automatically picked up a comb and ran it through my hair, staring blankly at my reflection in the glass, at a loss to know what I ought to do. Colin—and Cassie Hayter. Scarcely possible to imagine a more ill-assorted couple. The connection was unpalatable, but inescapable...the direction in which Colin's walk last night had taken him...the wampum earrings at his flat, the envelope in Cassie's shop...I knew now why the writing had so shaken Harmony, and why she had spoken of not being able to trust Colin. It seemed highly probable that his relationship with Cassie had been the cause of their broken engagement. In that case, how to explain her wish to go into partnership with Cassie? I would have felt happier if I could believe she really did wish that.

A door was banging, offbeat, irritating, somewhere along the corridor. I jumped up and went to shut it, and found it was the door of Lois's room. Someone had been in since I left it last night, for I was sure I had secured it firmly. Curiosity prompted me to enter again. I stood for a moment—what was it about this room, its atmosphere? I opened cupboards and drawers, all of which were empty, save for a few various oddments. What had Rowena been burning in here? Turning, I saw what I had missed the first time: a door flush with the panelling behind the bed, obvious now because it hadn't been firmly pressed home. It stuck when I pulled, then gave, and I was looking into what appeared to be a small boxroom, a repository for old trunks and boxes, wedged in between this and the previous bedroom. A deep, square woven basket with handles either side stood beside a stack of suitcases, and I saw at once it was full of what I suspected to be yet more of the papers I had spent the morning poring over. No wonder Lois had found it expedient to give in! Lifting a thick wodge of them, I saw they were indeed more bills and letters, piled on top of a stack of leatherbound ledgers, most likely housekeeping accounts. I had noticed their omission among the papers downstairs and assumed them to have been kept separately. Whatever businesslike qualities he lacked in other directions, Ralph, a typical Stonor, had been a stickler for keeping an eye on where the money went.

I opened one of the books. There on the first page in Ralph's distinctive, difficult writing, I read *Time Remembered,* a novel by Ralph Franklin Stonor. September, 1935.

I skimmed the first book quickly. It didn't seem to me, even as a rough draft, to be a very promising manuscript; a longwinded narrative into which many of Ralph's personal opinions and viewpoints were inserted as asides. A glance at the rest of the books showed them to be a continuation of the first. It was indeed a magnum opus, and my first impulse was to stuff the books back into the basket where I'd found them. Also, boring and tedious as it was to me, the novel had presumably meant a lot to my grandfather; it didn't seem right to pry into his private dreams.

Then something about one of those first-person viewpoints caught my eye, and all scruples vanished abruptly. I sat down on one of the boxes, prepared to go back to the beginning. Of course! Grandfather Ralph was at it again. These asides were never in fact intended to be included as part of the novel, they were simply random jottings of the sort he had dashed off so often on the papers downstairs, notes which had occurred to him as he was writing his manuscript. Only these were no mere scribbles. In this, his secret book, they amounted to a diary-like record of events, and his private thoughts and observations on them. I could no more have stopped myself from reading on when I saw my mother's name than I could have stopped breathing...

"I watched them again today, as I watched them every day," he wrote. "Lydia, our child of light. She dances like a wave of the sea, curtsies for approbation, and then smiles. The sun is in her smile, her every gesture. And my darling, my plain, sad, hesitant Ellen, watches too, silently, enviously, her heart in her eyes when Lydia goes to sit on her mother's lap, pouts prettily and puts her lips to be kissed. Ellen however hesitates to do the same, afraid of a rebuff where none is likely to come. Whatever her natural partiality, Isabella endeavours to favour neither one nor the other. I am afraid she does not always succeed. She is impatient with Ellen's slowness and reserve, which she tries to cover up with a strained kindness the child all too easily recognises. Ellen, Ellen! You must learn to put yourself forward, to show your talent for love and affection. Perhaps you are right to fear. Life will not be kind to you, my darling. Your feelings and emotions run too deep for comfort in this shallow world."

The novel began again, dull and plodding. The little room was hot and stuffy, my clothes stuck to my back and my tingling expectations did nothing to cool me down, but I read on with mounting excitement, running my eyes quickly over the ensuing pages, skipping until I came to the diary bits, undated, spasmodic, over the long years it had taken my grandfather to fill the books. And I blessed him for his secrecy, or circumspection, in hiding this rich treasure between the covers of his unborn novel. Had he not done so, had anyone else suspected what was hidden here, they would surely have removed it before I had chanced on it.

I tried to read slowly, to savour each word as if I were eating a rare and delicate dish, but my eyes raced ahead. Swiftly I began to put together the story of the two sisters as they grew up. Lydia, my mother, pretty, a little spoiled perhaps, but loved and popular, with brains as well as beauty, overshadowing her gauche, shy elder sister. The one as she grew up trailing glory and boyfriends behind her, the other drawing more and more into her shell, only becoming her true, gentle self when she was with her father.

Richard was mentioned often, too. An obvious extrovert. His father recorded with pleasure his success at sports; less enthusiastically, his lack of academic attainment, but always hopeful that Richard would join him at the bank, a hope eventually realised. He became engaged, then married, and Ralph's sole worry seemed to be his son's extravagance. Yet how strange it was that he never seemed to have felt as closely involved with his only son as he did with his daughters.

At this point, I became aware that I was hearing a booming noise reverberating from downstairs—the dinner gong, warning that the meal would be served in fifteen minutes. The sun had moved from this side of the house now and the tiny, stuffy room, lit only by a small window, was filled with shadows. My back ached with sitting on the upturned box, my eyes burned with trying to decipher Ralph's handwriting. Rivers of perspiration ran between my shoulder blades. I had been here very nearly five hours.

All the same, I was sorely tempted to ignore the gong. How could I leave all this, go downstairs and join the others filled with this boiling excitement, act as if I were not on the verge of discovering just what I had come to Stonor's Point for? For a minute longer, I sat there biting my lips. Then I grabbed the whole dusty armful of books and carried them along to my room, stuffed them into the back of my wardrobe, had a bath to beat all records for time, and was downstairs, only fractionally late, for dinner.

The hot bright weather had turned heavy and sultry, and the meal was served in the dining-room, which was cooler than outdoors, the French windows wide to the murmurous sound of the sea below.

'You are looking very pleased with yourself, cousin Charlotte. What ghastly secrets have you been uncovering today?' Sebastian remarked as I took my seat beside him.

I was saved from answering his typically flippant comment by Isabella. 'If that is what Charlotte is expecting, then she is bound to be sadly disappointed.' Her glance, her slight smile, rested on me as she spoke.

'Oh come,' Sebastian went on, unabashed. 'Why otherwise would anyone want to go delving into all those musty old papers?'

'Musty old papers—Stonor papers,' she said, coldly putting him down, 'do have a certain importance for posterity.'

Sebastian raised his eyebrows, while Max stood up to pull out a chair for Rowena, even later than I was. 'We will have the gong rung louder,' Isabella remarked, her voice heavy with sarcasm. 'Evidently it is not being heard.'

'I've been helping in the kitchen with preparations for tomorrow. It's a big house, and Mary and Mrs Roscoe can't do everything unaided.' I was more than pleased to hear a note of asperity in Rowena's voice, for once.

'They are not expected to. Extra help has been engaged for tomorrow,' Isabella returned, but she had the grace to look slightly ashamed. A moment later, she said, 'Thank you for having the photographs put back,' and, giving Rowena a totally unexpected smile, went composedly on with her dinner. Rowena, overcome, bent over her lobster salad.

We sat around the long polished table as the meal continued, the lamplight gleaming on heavy crystal and old silver, seven people keeping up a superficially civilised conversation that touched no one, gave no clue to the separate preoccupations of us all. We had spent the day separately, too, following our own interests. Was that the usual pattern of these birthday gatherings, putting in an appearance for form's sake, observing the proprieties for a few days in obedience to Isabella's wishes?

Had it always been like this? Had my mother once sat here thinking the very same things? That sense of déjà vu, the feeling of my mother's presence was almost overwhelming tonight. My thoughts flew at once back to the diary, to her and to Ellen. My aunt. More than a name to me now, a person related to me by blood and genes and inheritance...

Max reached silently for my glass and filled it with ruby warmth. Above the rim of his own glass his eyes met mine in a silent toast. What was it about this calm, self-assured man that drew me to him, yet made me confused and afraid? Was it that passion that I had glimpsed that ran underneath, damped down yet strong as fire?

He came to me when we had finished dinner and drew me to a corner of the terrace. 'Sebastian was right, you have found out something, haven't you?' he said without preamble.

'How do you know?'

'You look lit up with excitement. I've never seen you look like that before.'

But you could, Max, oh, you could.

I said, 'Yes, I think I have,' and told him as much as I thought was safe, which was that I had found an old diary which spoke of my mother's childhood. I too was learning to be deep and devious.

'Pack it in, Charlotte,' he said shortly when I'd finished. 'All that's been buried for thirty years. Don't rake it up.'

We'd been down this road before. 'No, I can't do that,' I told him steadily.

'You mean you won't.'

'All right then. I won't.'

He looked steadily at me, then Isabella could be heard asking if we wanted coffee. Abruptly, he walked over to fetch it, and when he returned, I'd prudently taken a seat next to Rowena.

I finished my coffee as quickly as I could, made my excuses and went along to the study to collect the writing materials I needed to make notes as I read the diaries, to work out when things had happened. Ralph had never bothered with mundane details such as dates.

As I went along the carpeted corridor, past the alcove where the telephone was, I saw Harmony using it. 'I know, I know I promised,' she was saying, her voice high and agitated and perhaps carrying further than she knew. 'I will let you know, only please, please don't do anything until I do. I'll ring you later,' she finished hurriedly, seeing me. 'Yes, of course I will.'

The receiver rattled as she put it back on its stand, and she threw me a questioning look, assessing what I'd heard. All through dinner she had seemed nervously on edge. She and Colin were still at loggerheads, and all Isabella's attempts to draw them into conversation with one another had failed. I said to her, 'Can you spare me a minute or two? Come into the study.'

She hesitated, then followed me. I opened the study door and stood stock still.

'Glory, what's happened?' she demanded, almost falling over me.

'Your guess is as good as mine.'

I had admittedly left the study that afternoon in what, to the casual observer, might have seemed like disorder, but the piles of papers dispersed around the room had in fact been reasonably well-organised. They weren't now. They had been arbitrarily swept up and shuffled together, then thrown on to the floor in a great, loose, untidy heap, almost as if waiting for a match to be set to them.

'Oh, Charlotte, this is wild! And you had them all sorted.'

'More or less.'

'Oh, Charlotte!' she said again, her eyes wide and frightened. 'Who's done this? What's happening around here? Things are falling apart—it never used to be like this.' Her voice shook, and I saw she was almost on the verge of tears.

'Hey, look, it's not that bad. It's going to be a bore, but not much more than another morning's work to re-sort the lot. It seems a pretty pointless sort of thing to have done, but no need to get upset about it. Forget it...that was Cassie you were talking to just now, wasn't it?'

'Cassie?' She jumped. 'Oh, oh yes, I guess so.'

'She's been upsetting you. Do you want to tell me why?'

There was a panic-stricken look about her for a minute, then she said in a low, dispirited voice, 'It isn't only Cassie. I asked Max this afternoon. He seemed in an approachable mood, so I took the bull by the horns...I wish I hadn't, he was really heavy. He refused to let me have any of my money, and he told me I wasn't on any account to approach Grandmother.'

'Oh dear. But predictable, wasn't it? Did he say why?'

'He doesn't like Cassie. Oh, he made

a lot of hassle about finishing what I've started, graduating, all that sort of ho-hum, but basically that's what it amounts to.'

'I suppose you should be glad he takes his responsibilities so seriously.'

She gave me a reproachful stare, as well she might. I was mouthing platitudes. 'I should've known you'd take his side. You don't want to get the wrong side of him—you're halfway in love with him, aren't you? There's no need to get uptight about it. He fancies you as well. In fact, I wouldn't drop dead with shock if he'd got his eye on you for the second Mrs Remmick.'

'That isn't funny,' I said coldly. She couldn't know just how unfunny it was. 'He hardly knows me, let alone fancies me, as you so elegantly put it. And in any case, he's still in love with the first Mrs Remmick.'

'My,' she mocked, 'don't you know anything? In love with Lois he was not! He *hated* her.'

There was a reverberating silence. 'Even supposing I believed that, how do you know?' I said, reluctant to ask, yet unable not to. 'Why should he hate her?'

Harmony shrugged. 'Just take your pick.

But I guess the main reason was she could never leave any man alone.' Her young, ingenuous face was all at once hard and condemning, closed up in the way I had seen before when she spoke of Lois. 'But I don't want to talk about that. Let's get back to me.'

'Yes. We have got off the point, haven't we?' I said, relieved to be let off the hook. Was it possible Max thought of me in the way Harmony suggested? I'd never before had to ask myself that question in relation to any man. I'd always known; I'd assumed one always did know if any mutual attraction existed. Well, be honest. After last night I knew only too well how strong the physical pull between us was. It was the other unspoken connections, the quickening of interest he aroused in me and the dozens of different ways he showed his own interest, that made the difference. It was my turn to panic now, and I said quickly to Harmony, 'Yes, well, what *is* to be done about you?'

I really couldn't think. It seemed to me there were too many unspoken reservations, and paramount was the question of why she was forcing herself along a path she seemed reluctant to take. I said slowly, 'Will you tell me the truth, Harmony? Has Cassie Hayter some hold over you?'

Her head jerked up. 'What makes you think that?'

'It's Colin, isn't it? And Cassie—'

I got no further, stopped short at the sight of her face. 'How—how did you find that out?' she whispered, stricken. Before I could frame a reply, she went on, 'No, no, don't tell me—I don't want to know, I don't want to know anything!' She grabbed my wrist, her eyes enormous, dilated more by the lenses of her glasses. 'You have to promise me you won't mention it to anyone else, not ever—his career would be ruined...his *life!*'

Colin's life ruined because of a liaison with Cassie? It sounded like something out of a Victorian novel.

Without saying anything more, she spun out of the room. I could hear flying footsteps down the hall, and when I glanced out of the window I saw her hurrying round the corner of the house.

For a while I was tempted to forget it, to let things sort themselves out. For about ten minutes, I aimlessly sorted out some of the jumbled papers, then, with a sigh, I followed her.

I went along the path she had taken and found it led through the kitchen gardens to the greenhouse beyond, and then to something looking like a Victorian birdcage in wrought iron, glassed in and built on to the side of the house. I caught a glimpse of her white dress through the windows, and went inside.

The steamy heat hit me like a blow as I went in, the jungle-like impression strengthened by the luxuriant foliage that was there to provide the right conditions for the orchids which grew everywhere. Exotic specimens clung like leeches to the bark of trees, festooned themselves along branches, sent out long spurs and sometimes breathtaking cascades of blossom. Somewhere in the centre a fountain played, jetting a stream of water up through the greenish gloom right to the ceiling. Iron pathways, green with moss, warm and moist from the ancient central heating pipes underneath, wound in mazelike formation, banked with foliage to the roof.

As I moved along, I caught glimpses of Harmony at the end of the building, talking to Roscoe. I made my way towards her, several times missing my direction and coming to a dead end. Then, between the dripping branches of some tropical tree, I saw her again. The man she was talking to was Colin, not Roscoe. Just as I saw this, the fountain stopped, evidently on a time switch, and in the silence their angry voices carried clearly.

'...into this mess,' Colin was saying.

'Oh, come *on!* You'll be denying ever having an affair with her, next.'

It seemed to be my day for eavesdropping on Colin's secret encounters. I should have left, in the best British tradition. I stayed, and listened as hard as I could, and heard Colin saying, 'I'm not denying it—I never have, but it's not as you think. The woman simply threw herself at me. It was more than flesh and blood could stand.'

Harmony made noises of disbelief and Colin, sounding desperate, said, 'After she persuaded that bloke to lend me his flat she seemed to think she had a right to pester me. I did everything I could to fend her off—ignored her, wrote and threatened to tell—'

'Sure, you ran away until you caught her!'

'Oh God, why won't you try to

understand? Think who she was! I had my career to think of!'

'You and your career! And look where it's got us.'

Silence. I was pleased she was giving him a hard time. He deserved it. My arm brushed against a creeper as I leaned forward to hear, releasing a heady, pervasive scent. Then, rough and menacing, Colin spoke again. 'Not any longer. There's only one way to fix her sort, once and for all.'

'Colin!' Harmony's voice was sharp and strident. 'Don't *say* things like that.'

A longer silence. I raised my head and what I saw through the stems of the tree made me turn and tiptoe out. Though they wouldn't have heard me if I'd worn hobnailed boots.

'Max? Why, I believe he's out on the terrace. He said he had some reading to catch up on, and he wanted to do it undisturbed.'

It was Sebastian, the first person I saw in the hall on my way in, lounging with his feet up on the table in the small alcove beneath the stairs where we'd taken tea the first day. 'But I daresay if it's important—'

he added, giving me a conjecturing look.

'Not really. I won't disturb him for more than a minute.'

I could feel his eyes following me as I crossed the hall and went into the dining-room. Outside the far door, on the terrace, Max was sitting writing in the last of the light. He put down his notepad at once and jumped up to pull a chair out for me. 'Let me get another glass and you can join me in a drink.'

'No thanks. I won't keep you long. I just wanted a word with you about Harmony.'

'Oh. I hope you haven't come to tell me,' he said very quickly, 'that you've been encouraging her in this mad scheme she told me about this afternoon?'

'Why should you think that?'

'Seems the sort of thing you might do. A blow for women's independence and all that,' he said, offhand, but he was alert for my reply.

I said shortly, 'I'm sorry you've such a poor opinion of my judgement. I'm as much against that idea as you are.'

He bent a long, considering look on me, slowly replaced by the smile that so lit up and changed his face. 'I'm sorry. I guess

I'm a mite scratchy on the subject. She threatened to go to Isabella, and I didn't want that to happen and upset her.'

I had to fight against that smile, what it could do to me. More sharply, more unfairly than I had intended, I said, 'It's always Isabella with you, isn't it? Harmony can be upset, too.'

He took a long drink. Leaning back in his chair, he said, 'There's something I think you should know. She ordered me not to tell you this, but I believe I'm justified in disobeying in the circumstances. Your grandmother has a bad heart condition. I don't want to alarm you unnecessarily, but it wouldn't take much to kill her at her age. She could go just like that. Coming here has already been more of a strain than she cares to admit.'

It became immediately clear now why she had been comparatively subdued for the last couple of days, content for the most part to rest, to spend her time reading, sitting on the balcony outside her bedroom. It was shattering to think what that single outburst against Rowena the other night might have done to her. I supposed she herself might have belatedly realised this, and that was why she had been very nearly agreeable to Rowena since. It explained, too, Max's continuing care and solicitude for her, and perhaps why he hadn't opposed her coming here. Thwarting Isabella at any time wasn't something one undertook lightly.

'That's bad.' We hadn't known each other long enough to have come close. She had done nothing in our brief acquaintance to endear herself to me. I was amazed to find a hard lump in my throat that made it difficult to speak.

'She accepts it,' Max said quietly. 'She's had a good long life—and there are worse ways to die, believe me.'

I swallowed hard. 'This business with Harmony wouldn't help, I see that now, but she—Harmony, that is—worries me.'

Something about that overheard conversation was bothering me, too. Something had been said that I hadn't latched on to, something, I felt sure, which ought to have had meaning for me. 'I'm afraid she's going to do something stupid.'

'We all do that from time to time, even when we're old enough to know better.' But again came that wary, observant glance.

'That isn't to say we shouldn't be prevented.'

'True, true. But there's more to all this than you realise. Don't get yourself involved. You could make it worse for her, and land yourself—and other people—in some serious trouble. Leave me to deal with Harmony, hm?'

A lot of bad things had happened, were still happening, to this family, here in this house. I could feel it in the walls, in the air, threatening to disrupt the lives of people I liked. I couldn't sit by and do nothing. 'There's something perhaps *you* don't know. I think Cassie Hayter is blackmailing Harmony, perhaps Colin too.'

Now I had certainly succeeded in gaining his undivided attention. 'Go on.'

'For a start, I don't believe Harmony really wants to get involved with Cassie.' I went on to tell him everything that had made me suspicious, starting with my visit to Colin's flat and ending with what I'd just overheard. 'But I haven't got the connections, yet. I don't see how his having an affair with Cassie comes into it. If Harmony broke their engagement because of that—'

'No.' Across his face flickered that strange, withdrawn look. Before going on, he drained his glass, then stood up and leaned against the terrace railing, his back to the sea. Palms flat on the top rail, looking directly at me, he said, 'They broke up because Harmony found out Colin was having an affair with my wife.'

'With *Lois?*' How could I have been so crass? Why did I always have to rush into things so unthinkingly? What was there to say? 'I'd never have dreamed—if I'd even suspected—'

'I wouldn't have told you if I thought you had.' He smiled faintly, though the smile failed to reach his eyes. 'Don't feel too bad about it. It wasn't the first time, and it wouldn't have been the last. They never went on long, those affairs of hers. This one was all but over when Harmony heard them having a big argument. That was how she found out. Though I don't suppose Harmony's aware I know, that I had it straight from my dear wife herself. She rather enjoyed telling me.'

'Max. I'm so sorry.'

'Don't be. We were all washed up, anyway.'

I could hear again, in my head, Harmony saying it was here, at Stonor's Point, where things had gone terribly wrong last year...and Colin—dear God, what a fool I'd been! He and Harmony had been talking about his affair with *Lois*. But...*I'll fix her, once and for all*, Colin had said. And that must have meant Cassie.

'Poor devil,' Max was saying, 'I don't suppose he had a chance. He was infatuated, they all were. That doesn't mean I wasn't pretty sick about it.'

For an ambitious man, I thought, Colin had been playing a risky game. And Cassie had found out—and threatened to tell Max, not knowing he already knew. I saw what Harmony meant. It could still have damaged Colin, even though Lois was dead. But no. That wouldn't do, not quite. For one thing, I couldn't see Colin submitting to blackmail over a thing like that. I got up and went to join Max. We turned round, elbows on the rail, to look down at the sea, glittering in the fading light.

'I'm not blaming her, any more than myself. We should never have gotten married. We were both too young, too opposite. It doesn't matter now...it's past. You don't want to hear about all that.'

'Yes, I do,' I said, facing him. 'If you want to tell me, that is.'

He too straightened up, looking taut and strained, and put his hands on my shoulders, giving me a deep, hard look. 'Oh, I want to, Charlotte. I want you to know everything. No secrets between us—even the bad things. That's important. Do you understand me?'

I could feel myself starting to tremble, emotionally stirred by the racing under-currents passing between us, yet with that deep, uneasy premonition again shivering inside me. 'Go on, please,' I whispered.

'It isn't a pretty story.'

'That doesn't matter.'

'Impetuous Charlotte! Better reserve your judgement until you know.' He took his hands from my shoulders and turned to face the sea. 'I was only just out of medical school when we married. I guess I fell in love with the way she looked. I hadn't even begun to know the person she was, any more than she knew me, that's for sure. Then, for the first time, I found I wasn't in control of my own life any more. Things had always gone as I'd planned, medical school, my career...' His voice had dropped. The low tones sounded strange, almost savage. 'Then I married Lois, and found that one person, *one person*, could turn my life upside down. I couldn't help myself, I couldn't help her.'

In front of us, a seabird swooped in a silver downward arc, giving a long, mewling cry. 'Do you really want to hear the rest?' His face was harsh, the skin taut across the bones of his cheeks. There were beads of sweat on his forehead.

I was more frightened than I had ever been in my life. What was he trying to tell me? With every fibre of my being, I didn't want to know, yet I had to listen, like a moth drawn to singe its wings at the candle.

The moment of silence stretched between us, almost to breaking point, and then there was a loud crash, and the terrace was alive with shards of flying glass.

10

Max stood in the centre bay of my room, looking at the space in the empty frame where the window should have been. He had been nearer than he knew when he had warned me that the window cords might be suspect. The room was full of people, attracted from all points of the compass by the noise.

'You surely are the most accident-prone person I have ever met, Charlotte! I cannot understand why those cords should break like that. Roscoe tests them regularly.' Isabella was clearly more irritated than upset, defensive of her well-maintained property.

'The strain of the window being opened and shut after all this time must have been too much,' Max said. Below, Mrs Roscoe was sweeping broken glass from the terrace and could be heard exclaiming at what a miracle it was nobody had been hurt. 'You might easily have had your fingers trapped when you were opening the window, Charlotte, so it's as well they broke when they did.'

'Yes,' I said, staring at the white-painted frame. 'It is, isn't it?'

'They were frayed; it's a natural break,' he stated, very firmly, as if the thought had crossed his mind, too, that it might not have been.

'What will you do tonight?' Rowena, more worried than I was, fussed around making sure no splinters had been left on the carpet. The brush in her hands actually trembled.

'Don't make such a pother, Ro,' Sebastian drawled, supporting himself by the doorpost. 'They can surely be left until tomorrow. In this heat, we shall all be sleeping with the windows wide, anyway.

It was left like that, after I had finally got rid of them by telling them I was dead tired and longing for bed. Max put his hand briefly on my shoulder as he left, that calm, reassuring touch that was his trademark. 'Tomorrow, Charlotte?' he said in a low voice that was a promise to resume our violently interrupted conversation. And after a thoughtful pause, 'Take care.'

Immediately they had gone, I took the key from my handbag and unlocked the wardrobe. The diaries, undisturbed, were still there.

I made myself ready for bed, then settled into a chair and opened the books at the point where I'd so reluctantly left off, but now, when I was alone with all the uninterrupted hours of the night before me, I was restless, perversely finding it difficult to begin again, to project myself backwards in time, to remove myself from what had happened today.

The words stared meaninglessly up at me from the page...

What I hadn't told anyone was that I had left that window wide open, not with the bottom section up, but with the top one down, so that there could have been no weight on the cords to cause them to break. Unless someone else had pushed the two sections up from the bottom.

And that was a thing to think about...that and the brownish smear that looked extraordinarily like blood on the side of the frame. Which might, to be sure, have been there some time, unnoticed; but wasn't it too much of a coincidence that the cords had snapped just as I was speaking with Max on the terrace below?

With an effort, I forced my attention

back to the closely-written pages, making myself ignore the insidious unease lurking on the edge of consciousness, and gradually what Grandfather Stonor had to tell me of other lives lived out here and in Boston over thirty years ago succeeded in grasping, then holding, my attention.

Here indeed was a side to my mother I had never even suspected could exist: Lydia, dating young men, riding, swimming, the belle of every dance she attended. I tried to imagine her...1940s scrubbed-fresh face, shining-haired, bobby-soxed. And Ellen, poor Ellen, defeated before she began, so eager to please, so anxious for affection. For Ellen, read Rowena, I thought... Was this then where Isabella's impatience with Rowena began, why she had been so ready to believe the worst of her? Seeing in her the reincarnation of her mother, was Isabella assailed with guilt because she had been unable to love her as much as Lois/Lydia?

A solitary girl, Ellen seemed to have had few interests. Unlike her sister, with her high-school dates, dances and tennis parties, she seemed content to shop endlessly for clothes she had little occasion to wear, to seek out additions to her collection of blown glass animals. She drew and painted a little, read a lot. Her father worried about her aimless existence, about her future. Maybe it was this which caused him to write: 'Today, Isabella told me she had spoken with Ellen about George Allot. As he is a second cousin, and not entirely penniless, I can put forward no objection, none that would count with Isabella. His background and qualifications are impeccable, and he is more than willing to marry my daughter, as indeed he should be. Some day, through her, he will be a rich man. I have searched my conscience and I hope this is not why I cannot like him. Parental jealousy is never pretty. He smiles too much, and Ellen is dazzled. He is the only one who has offered for her, yet she insists she knows what she is about and will accept him. For a moment, she faltered when I asked her if she thought he loved her. Then she asked me an unanswerable question: *Did you love my mother when you married her?*'

Ralph's handwriting became more indecipherable than ever at this point, and it was some time before I could make out the next passage... 'I love Isabella now with all my heart. I believe she loves me, too, as I her, with every fault. It wasn't so when we married; there were storms, until the years brought children, a respect for each other, peace...and finally love. Whether parallels can be drawn with Ellen's case, I find myself too involved to say.'

I was very moved, and for a moment put the books to one side, got up and went to stand in front of the glassless window. Outside was deep silence, except for the sea, the everlasting, incidental music of Stonor's Point, whispering and curling at the foot of the cliff.

Last night, down there, I had been wakened to a realisation of what Max could mean to me; tonight, we had taken several long steps forward. And I was afraid. At the lack of will I had shown, at the readiness with which I'd been prepared to step right into whatever awaited me with him. Who knows what I might not have let myself in for if the window hadn't broken? Max Remmick was a different proposition from the others, who had understood. He would settle for nothing less than total commitment. It was time I left, went home, moved on. It wasn't yet too late.

I had in any case almost fulfilled my promise to get at the reasons for my mother's flight. I had the strung-up feeling which I was certain meant I was nearing the end of my search, now that the layers of secrecy were being stripped off like the skins of an onion.

Outside, one of the dogs barked, a deep baying that echoed into the night. Shivering, I drew back and returned to the diaries.

The novel began again on the next page and went on for some time, and the diary entries didn't begin again until after Ellen was married to George Allot. Then I began to notice that the novel passages were becoming less frequent. Finally, all pretence at writing it was dropped. Reading was easier now, mostly of humdrum day-to-day events. There was mention of Lois's birth, and a year later Rowena's. Richard's divorce overshadowed several pages, but fast crowding it out came Ralph's fears concerning Ellen's marriage, too. His earlier doubts about George Allot seemed to have been well founded. 'Why was I so weak as to allow this marriage?' he reproached himself continually. 'He has not, as I knew in my heart he could not, made her happy. If only she were here at home again, by my side, where we could talk, and I could comfort her. I tell myself it is in the natural course of events for a daughter to leave home. When Lydia leaves for Vassar in the fall I shall miss her sorely, but her going will not leave a gap that cannot be filled.'

And then, halfway through the next volume, I read: "George Allot has volunteered for service with the U.S. Army. He is being sent for immediate training. My Ellen and her little daughter are to come home and live with us again.'

I rubbed my eyes. It was after two, and I was so tired I could scarcely see to read, but I knew I had to go on. I was on the last of the ledgers now, and, keyed up with nervous excitement, I knew how near I was to learning the truth. Grandfather had spared little in his out-pourings. I turned the page and found—nothing.

All the remaining pages in this last volume were blank. I was forced to admit, in an agony of disbelief, that this must have been the point where he died. I checked, and it roughly fitted with my calculations. How bitterly, cruelly frustrating, to have got so far and to have the final truth withheld. I snapped the book together, holding it upright on my knee, choking down a disappointment so deep I could have cried. It was then that I noticed a looseness along the spine of the book. Between the last entry and the blank pages at the end of the book, a whole section had been removed.

The morning brought little relief from the heat of the previous day. The sun still shone brassily from a sky of hard, brilliant blue, and I slept late, thereby missing the chance of a swim before breakfast, unlike Max whom I saw from my window swimming to the shore in an expert crawl, and running up the beach. There wasn't any set time for breakfast, but I was afraid that if I waited until after I'd been swimming it would have been cleared—and I was very hungry. I had been able to eat scarcely anything at dinner the night before.

The winscot panelling in the breakfast-room had been painted white. Above it a collection of pretty china was displayed on walls of a sunny yellow; dark furniture stood on a pale Chinese carpet. Cream shantung curtains, partly drawn, fluttered at the long windows, keeping the room cool. I saw that everyone had almost finished when I came in, but there were hot dishes on the sideboard. I helped myself to ham and scrambled egg, decided to be courageous and not fish out the pineapple and strawberries which garnished it.

Max came to pour me hot coffee from the percolator and to replenish his own cup. He was already tanning. His eyes looked vividly blue, his hair was still damp. 'You look tired. Didn't you sleep well?'

'Too hot,' I answered with a quick smile, slipping into my seat at the table, where only my grandmother was missing, and Colin, his red hair alive with electricity from being rubbed dry, was trying to find a partner for a round of golf on the nearby course.

Declining politely, Max explained that he was going to collect his boat. 'Before you go, maybe you'll spare me half an hour?' he asked Colin, who said he would, and Max added: 'Why don't you ask Sebastian to have a round with you?'

'Wish I could,' answered Sebastian, quick with his excuses, 'but I reckon I pulled a muscle in my arm yesterday jacking up my car—and all to no avail, alas! I'm no mechanic. Have to get a garage to pick the damn thing up this morning.'

Rowena pushed her chair back abruptly. 'Excuse me, I have things to do,' she said, and left the room.

Max gave Sebastian a quick look, 'Better let one of us see that arm.' But Sebastian hastily waved the suggestion away, saying it was nothing much.

Harmony was groaning at all this energy. 'Me, I'm for the nearest patch of shade with a book and a pitcher of lemonade. This heat kills me.'

Her reconciliation with Colin wasn't being made public. They sat at opposite sides of the table, avoiding one another's eye; but there seemed to be a suppressed febrile excitement about her—even her insatiable appetite appeared to have deserted her, as though some inner excitement provided the nourishment she needed. She had hardly touched her breakfast. 'How about you, Charlotte? I suppose you'll be cooping yourself up in that old study again this morning?' The words were polite enough, but I could tell she was still slightly cool with me over last night.

Dismissing the thought of the shambles awaiting me in the study, I said I might walk to the village and browse around. In fact, I wanted time to work out my next move. Although last night I'd been shattered by the discovery that those diary pages were missing, by this morning I was thinking more clearly. Their removal had proved beyond doubt that they had contained something revealing enough to need concealment. If they'd been taken out recently—last night, by the person who'd been in my room?—I had at least a sporting chance of finding out by whom. I looked around the table. No one wore a plaster or bandage, or showed evidence of a recent cut. Perhaps that had been too much to expect.

'I need presents to take back home, and there seemed to be a good selection in the village,' I said. 'I liked the look of several things in Cassie's shop.'

Maybe I wasn't yet functioning in top gear this morning, so perhaps I didn't quite succeed in making my announcement as spontaneous as I had hoped. Though I could have imagined the strained silence that followed what I said, the feeling of some guarded, unspoken exchange between Colin and Harmony.

Max paused in the act of stirring his coffee. 'Don't go. By the look of you, you'd be better catching up on some sleep.'

He was really repeating what he'd said last night—keep out of it, don't interfere—but I was thinking to myself that I'd been in the dark long enough, and that maybe a talk with Cassie Hayter wouldn't come amiss.

'I'm not so old,' I said rather briskly, 'that I can't stand a few sleepless hours.'

'I guess I'd better come with you then.' Harmony sat back, elaborately casual. 'Make sure they don't try to sell you the Brooklyn Bridge and all.'

I assured her I wouldn't allow myself to be taken in. 'You stick to your lazy day, and I'll go on my own. I'm not good at concentrating when I'm with anyone else, and I've a list a mile long. But I'm going to swim first.'

'Then if everyone else is occupied, I'll just rest up and make myself beautiful for tonight.'

'Oh God,' Sebastian said. 'I'd almost managed to forget the Birthday. Well, let's get the charade over so we can all get back to Boston and our own lives.'

No one seemed to have anything to add to this and presently they began to drift out one by one. Max got up to leave, sketching a goodbye in a general way. He didn't spare me a glance as he left the room, at his most remote. He seemed to have forgotten, or, worse, not to care, that our conversation last night had been left uncompleted, hanging in the air. Perhaps he too felt the breaking of the window had been a reprieve. I pushed my plate away. I didn't seem hungry after all.

The coolness of the water was like a benison after the glaring heat of the beach. I swam for a while, floated and swam again, refusing to think, letting my body take over and make me blessedly relaxed. When I'd had enough, I pulled on my towelling beach dress, rubbed my hair rough dry and sat down for a while at the water's edge, my hands laced round my knees, until the sun had dried it completely. Then I slipped my sandals on and walked back through the soft sand towards the path.

About half-way up the steep incline, one of the big grey rocks moved. Then it growled and lifted its head. Showing its fangs, it stood up; a paw like a sledge-hammer lifted and reached forward. Without grace, but making up for it in speed, I retreated as far as the beach hut, and the Alsatian lay down again. Its eyes never left me.

I sat down on the sand again, and considered. The dog gave another warning growl low in its throat and was answered by its chum, the black one, higher up the path. My heart began to go like a bongo drum. If they stayed where they were, okay. I could stop here until someone came, even if I grilled like a sardine on a spit in the process. But if the dogs decided to come after me...

I looked at the cliffs, sheer from top to bottom. No dice. No question, either, of swimming around the rocks, facing the dangerous currents. I wasn't a strong enough swimmer to make it. The beach house. A flimsy wooden structure, rotten with age. They'd just huff and puff and blow it right down. And locked anyway, as I found when I stood up and reached out a hand to try the door. There only remained the chain-link fencing between Stonor's Point and the neighbouring property, jutting out into the sea along the rocks into which it had been driven. Only a couple of its ten feet visible above the rising tide at the further end.

I reckoned I might, in extremis, grip

with my fingers and bare toes and scale the fence, here where the sea hadn't yet reached, though I wasn't sure how quickly I could do this. Gingerly, I slipped off my sandals and with a cautious backward glance at the dogs took a few necessary steps, reached my hand up experimentally and threaded my fingers through the mesh. Before I could test my weight, a volley of barking sounded, and the dogs, both of them, crashed right down the path and on to the beach. I let go and turned to face them, spread like a fly against the fencing.

They waited, and lay down, one black, one grey, their great heads on their paws, at the bottom of the path. As long as I kept motionless, they stayed where they were. Every time I moved, they set up that furious barking. So maybe I should keep moving, like Simon said, a hand, a foot, anything to keep up the noise and bring someone to investigate. I was drenched with perspiration and the horrid feeling came to me that they might decide they'd had enough of stalking me and look for a little more fun. I reached for my sandals, the only weapon I had, lost my balance and fell, and they made a concerted rush.

And then I heard a beautiful, beautiful sound...a piercing whistle, and loose stones falling as someone slithered down the path. The dogs, scattering sand on my face, braked to a halt two feet from me and sat up, ears pricked. I called out. I doubt whether my rescuer heard me. My voice came out as a pitiful croak as at the bottom of the path emerged the green sparrow figure of Ewart Roscoe.

'Why, Miss Haigh, what goes on down here?'

He took in the situation at a glance, then commanded the dogs on ahead, following them, and I shakily brought up the rear. When we were at last walking on level ground again he said, with a sideways glance at me, 'Best come straight into the kitchen with me and let Mrs Roscoe or Miss McDermott fix you a drink or something. Guess you've had a pretty rough half hour.'

'I'm okay,' I said. But I wasn't, not really, inside. I felt cold and sick.

'Well I could sure use something. Scared the pants off me when I heard the dogs and saw you lying there. Put me right in mind of the night I found Mrs Remmick.'

'*You* found her?'

'Sure. I heard the dogs creating, and I found her there, stretched out on the rocks. So I fetched her husband, fast, him being a doctor and all, though I knew she was dead. If he'd stopped with her in the first place, might never have happened, but how was he to know? Must've happened right after he left.'

I stumbled against part of a fallen branch, almost lost my balance. 'What—what do you mean?'

'Why, they was down there together, two of 'em, about a half-hour earlier. Then I saw him come up through the woods and into the house. Later, the dogs started up their racket, same as now. Sure was weird feeling to see you lying there...that sort of thing isn't my idea of a joke.'

'It's not mine, either.' I threw a wary glance towards the dogs, obedient to his command, kept at a safe distance between us. 'I thought they weren't allowed to run loose.'

'They're not. Only at night, when everyone's in bed. How they got out this morning, Miss Haigh, is something I'd really like to know.'

Someone else would have liked to know,

too. Me. They hadn't only been let loose, they'd been set to guard me, I was sure.

Declining Roscoe's invitation—I didn't want to face anyone else yet—I went to my room, changed and went downstairs again and poured myself something that looked like whisky from a decanter on the dining-room sideboard. Taking it out on to the terrace, I drank it slowly, resisting the impulse to down it in one go, letting it and the sun gradually warm me through to my bones.

It was whisky, and its heat spreading through me finally stopped the shaking inside. I was feeling almost human again by the time I saw a shadow through the screen door: Rowena coming into the dining-room carrying a huge flower arrangement in a Chinese vase. Placing it on the floor in the corner, she stood back critically, then twitched a peony into a better position.

She jumped as if a squib had been set at her heels when I spoke to her. 'It's only me. You're very nervous.'

She came to join me, letting the screen door slam behind her on its spring. 'I didn't see you out there. Are you all right? I've just heard what happened on the shore. You must have been scared...but the dogs wouldn't have hurt you.' She stood holding on to the back of the chair opposite. 'Roscoe must have forgotten to close their compound.'

'Or someone freed them, someone who knew how to handle them. Which does rather narrow the choice.'

'I'm not sure I know what you're trying to say.'

'I'm saying somebody's trying very hard to harass me. They were loosed on me, those dogs. And last night all the papers I spent yesterday sorting were deliberately mixed up. My guess is, by the same person who tore the last few pages from Grandfather Stonor's diary so that I shouldn't see them.'

She sat down, heavily for so slender a woman, looking paler than I felt. 'How in the *world* do you know *that?*'

'The diary? I found it yesterday. Was it those pages you were burning in Lois's room the night before last? Or maybe you have a key to my wardrobe?'

'No! I mean no, I didn't tear them out!' She looked frightened, then she added defiantly, 'I was burning an old poem of mine, if you must know, from a school magazine. These things are kind of embarrassing to look at, years later. I don't know how it had got in there.'

I was inclined to believe her. Such a crazy explanation had to be true. 'So you didn't jumble up the papers in the study, and you didn't set the dogs on me either, I suppose?'

'Why do you keep on about the dogs? I wouldn't do a thing like that. Okay,' she said, defiant again, 'so maybe I did disarrange the papers, but it wasn't spite. I was looking for—something, and they all got so hopelessly muddled...I was going to tell you and apologise and then I thought if I made it even worse, it might discourage you.'

'I don't discourage that easily,' I said, wondering why Rowena should want to. 'Who did tear those pages out then? Isabella?'

'No. No, it couldn't have been her.' She leaned back, closing her eyes for a second. 'I think it was Lois.'

'Lois?'

'I've looked and looked, everywhere. I've never even found the diary, never mind the pages. She must have destroyed the lot.

That's—what we fell out about, the day she died.'

'It wasn't over the necklace, then?'

'Necklace? What necklace?' She looked perfectly blank.

'It doesn't matter.' It had only been a thread of suspicion.

'We weren't fighting about any necklace. It was because she'd found this diary, and she was threatening to tell Grandmother what was in it, if—' She broke off, took cigarettes and lighter from her pocket and made a business of lighting one. I had a sharp impression she was playing for time, wondering exactly what to tell me, but in the end she said flatly, 'You might as well know the rest, I guess.'

'It might help.'

'She was extravagant, our cousin Lois,' she began abruptly. 'She used to spend money like it was going out of fashion, you know? Max gave her everything she wanted—clothes, jewellery, everything. But she wasn't satisfied, she always wanted more...she was talking about a yacht, a house on Palm Beach, for heaven's sake—as if he could afford a lifestyle like that! But naturally, *she* would have been able to afford it, when she inherited

Grandmother's money.' She drew deep on her cigarette, a displacement action that didn't quite conceal the bitterness that crossed her face.

She went on after a moment, more steadily. 'She started borrowing on the strength of that, speculating. And—well, for some peculiar reason, it seems she gave Sebastian quite a sum to invest for her. I don't know exactly the whys and wherefores, he doesn't talk about his business deals too much, you know what men are. I guess it's better that way anyway. I've my own business worries,' she said, holding on to her pride.

A startled expression crossed her face. '*What* was that you said just now about a necklace?'

I wished I hadn't been so quick to assume her quarrel with Lois had been about the necklace, because now I should have to tell her what Isabella had told me, though at least I could spare her Isabella's suspicions. To my relief, it was a controlled excitement she showed rather than any astonishment when she'd heard me out. 'Of course!' she exclaimed, almost to herself. 'That would be it, wouldn't it? Don't you see, it wasn't money Lois gave

Sebastian, but this necklace...she would have every chance to take it, and she was so impatient she wouldn't believe he couldn't dispose of something like that in a hurry—not if he wanted to get a good price...and yes, it was one whole lot of money she said he was owing her...'

I noticed how quickly she had accepted not only the idea of Lois as a thief, but also Sebastian's part in the affair. I thought this showed more clearly than anything she could have said that it wasn't the first time she'd been faced with his questionable activities. But I still couldn't see why Lois holding the diaries should bother Sebastian...only in so far as Rowena held the purse-strings and could get him off the hook with Lois...

'What was it that Ralph had written in his diary, Rowena,' I asked slowly, 'that concerned, you, to make you so afraid?'

'Nothing that could have hurt me, not now. It was Grandmother who would have been hurt. Something happened, a long time ago, that she's never known about, or even suspected. There's no knowing what it would have done to her if she'd been told. You know she has a heart condition?'

'So I've just learned.'

'Lois knew. And she didn't care,' she said savagely. 'She didn't give a damn that a sudden shock could be fatal, just so she could have her own little revenge on me.'

'But you cared.'

Her pale cheeks became suffused with colour. 'I would have done anything to prevent her doing such a cruel, mindless thing, yes.' Our eyes met across the table. 'Except *that.* I didn't kill her, Charlotte.'

'No.'

I waited until she'd finished her cigarette; as she ground it out she said, 'So that's that. Now you know.'

'But I don't know the half of it! You still haven't told me what was in the diary.'

She was calm enough now, standing, smoothing her skirt. 'I'm not going to,' she said, with as much decision as I'd ever seen in her.

'Because it concerns my mother, doesn't it?' Stung, I jumped up. 'Which makes me the very one who has every right to know.'

She did a very surprising thing. For Rowena incredible. Cupping my face in her long, delicate hands and looking earnestly at me, she said, 'There are reasons why I should like you to know, more than anything in the world. But those same reasons are why you mustn't know, ever.'

She dropped her hands and looked at them with a very strange expression. Then she gave me a wry, self-conscious smile and left me sitting at the table.

11

It was finally after lunch when I set off for Cassie's village. It turned out to be further away than I had remembered, distances being deceptive by car, and the oppressive stillness about the afternoon that made every step an effort told me, too late, that it hadn't been a good idea to refuse Harmony's offer of her car. I was like a wet rag by the time the little community huddled round the harbour came into sight below me.

I pushed on towards Cassie's boutique, walking the crowded length of the pier between the gift shops with their open doors and cheerful windows. Amongst them all, Cassie's door was closed like a fist. I knocked, rattled the knob, but it stayed shut. I looked for the "Back Soon" sign she had left when I'd been there before, with Harmony, but there was nothing pinned to the wooden planks of the door, or propped up in the window, either.

For no reason, I felt a crawling apprehension.

The faintest of breezes moved in from the sea, seagulls swooped and mewled overhead, a motor-boat chugged as, frustrated and undecided, I stood wondering whether to leave a note telling her I would come again, or whether the surprise tactics of an unannounced arrival would be better. I rummaged in my shoulder bag for ballpoint pen and paper to take note of the telephone number alongside her name on the signboard above the door. As I was writing it down, a woman came from the shop next door, the art gallery, Miranda Martell.

Eyeing me curiously, a thin middle-aged woman, her skin and hair bleached as if she'd been left out too long in the salt air, with faded blue eyes that nevertheless held a sharp curiosity, she enquired, 'You looking for Miz Hayter?'

'I was, but she doesn't appear to be in.'

'That's right. Man came visiting her this morning in a yellow Chevy—'

Colin's car. 'A red-haired man?'

'No, no. This guy was tall, with fairish hair. Distinguished-looking, I'd say.'

My heart jerked painfully. 'She went off with this man?'

'I didn't exactly see her, but that's what it looks like. Around noon, see, there's this delivery of some materials she'd ordered, ordered very special to be here at twelve, the truck driver said, but she wasn't here to take them. Real mad he was, but he wouldn't leave them without cash—you English?'

'Yes,' I said. 'And she didn't leave a message?'

The woman shook her head, her pale eyes narrowing. All her colour seemed to have gone into the lurid landscapes she sold. 'No, and that's not like her. She always leaves her key and a note, or tells me where she's going. You want me to tell her you called when she gets back?'

'No, I'll give her a ring. Goodbye—and thank you.'

'You're welcome.'

I felt her gaze follow me as I walked down the pier and turned my footsteps back up the road to Stonor's Point. Both energy and inclination for my ostensible present-buying had abruptly left me. As I reached the end of the pier I saw a man lounging against a shop window, reading a newspaper. He raised it in front of his face as I passed. But I recognised the suit. It belonged to Bernie Fisher—the man I thought of as 'The White Rabbit'.

I lay on my bed, in my mother's room, when I got back, depleted mentally and physically, but neither my lack of sleep the previous night nor my energetic and exhausting activities of today could make me rest. The events of the day were beginning to mount up to a dreadful significance, relentlessly forming themselves into a pattern. Staring at the ceiling, the beginnings of a headache behind my eyes, I masochistically listed my suspicions, beginning with Max's almost too opportune appearance that day when I'd nearly fallen into the traffic. Fallen? Pushed? The answer seesawed. The question nagged.

And then, this morning, those dogs. One had to believe that the purpose of them being sent down there was not to harm me, but to detain me—and that could only have been done by someone they were used to obeying. It was reasonable to assume that Max would have control over his wife's dogs—but then, perhaps anyone who knew the right commands would do. Don't make excuses, Charlotte! They had been sent there to keep me on the beach, to delay me from going to Cassie's shop until Max had had a chance to get there first.

More than ever I was convinced that Cassie Hayter had some strange liaison with all the people in this house. And now she was gone. Vividly I remembered Max saying at breakfast that he was going to pick up his boat...

I stirred restlessly. Imaginings that I would have dismissed as beyond the bounds of possibility before today crowded in on me, seeming to invest themselves with eerie implication. Like Roscoe's information that Max had been down there on the beach with Lois just before she died...and what was it that he himself had felt he must tell me last night before we were interrupted—and thought better of this morning? Had he been going to confess to—to having killed Lois?

I closed my eyes. No, no, and no!

My mind groped for the connection between my search for my mother's past and the events leading to Lois's death. Because it seemed certain to me now, irrevocably, inescapably, that there was a connection, that the information stored on the missing pages of the diary must in some way have given some clue to Lois's death. But Lois had taken those papers, before she died, and destroyed them.

Or someone else had, afterwards.

The room was stifling. I went to the window. The cords had been renewed, the glass replaced. I pushed it up to its widest extent and leaned out, trying to get a breath of air, but the heat lay like a lid, the sea looked flat and metallic in the lurid half light. Everything was still, waiting. I wondered if Max's boat was now moored down there, on the beach. Sounds from below told me that preparations were going well ahead for the evening: the party which I must attend as though nothing had happened. I must get ready. But first, I had to ring Cassie Hayter.

The large hall looked splendid and impressive as I passed through. Branches of candles had been set out, and already some were lit to relieve the flat heavy dullness of the late afternoon. The horses on the tapestry with their seated huntsmen seemed to have a life of their own, moving in procession in the flickering light. There were flowers everywhere in the house—no doubt Rowena's work—great scented sprays of blossom gathered from the garden and brought indoors.

In the small alcove off the hall which contained the telephone, I dialled Cassie's number for the second time since I had returned, and waited. A small window beside me overlooked the backyard. Outside, a caterer's van pulled in and several trays of canapes were brought into the house. I let the ringing tone continue for several minutes before putting the receiver back on its rest.

When I turned round, Harmony was waiting for me, nervously twiddling a strand of curly hair. 'Guess what?'

'You're engaged again.'

'Right! But how did you know?' Amazed and disconcerted.

'You could say I've been picking up signals.' I put my arm round her shoulders and squeezed. 'I'm so glad everything's turned out all right for you.'

Her bright, wide, embracing smile made her look as if the weight of the world had been taken from her. 'I didn't think it was so obvious,' she said ingenuously.

'And I'm not sure yet I deserve it, I've been so incredibly stupid. I really ought to have told you.'

The breakfast-room door was open. She went in and I followed, closing the door behind us. I went to the window-seat and she came and curled up beside me.

'You seem to have got the wrong impression about Colin—and Cassie. But it wasn't what you imagined with them. That wasn't why I broke our engagement. He—' She bent her head, the golden curls drooped, the glasses slipped and were pushed back, but she went on doggedly, determined to say what she had plainly rehearsed. I didn't interrupt her, didn't tell her I already knew what she thought was news to me. Then my interest focused, sharpened.

'I could have forgiven him that, I guess,' she was saying, working hard at believing it. 'Lois had that effect on men. But it was what I heard him saying to her. "I'll kill you," he said. "I'll kill you, I swear to God I'll kill you." That's what he said.' Her eyes widened and darkened with remembered shock. 'And then...that night...well, she died, didn't she?'

'Are you saying you believed Colin had murdered her?'

'Charlotte, what *else* was I to think? Oh, sure, it was dumb, but I suppose I was so mad at him I'd have believed anything.'

'Didn't you think to have it out with him?'

'I couldn't make myself talk about it. And it wasn't only me—it was both of us, refusing to discuss things, even to speak with one another. I mean, when Colin gets stubborn, he's something else! I just told him I knew about Lois and gave him his ring back. And he took it. He didn't know what I'd overheard, of course, not until Cassie told him, just about a week back.'

'Don't tell me—you confided in her and she started blackmailing you into becoming her partner. When you didn't move quick enough, she approached Colin?'

'You *have* been picking up signals!'

'Or putting two and two together.'

'She thought I was pretty naïve and she was right, too, but even I could see it wouldn't stop at a few thousand dollars invested in the shop. Trouble was, I couldn't see what else to do. I should've done what Colin did. He strung her along for a bit, but yesterday he more or less told her to do her worst.'

I'll never change my mind about you, Cassie. The words were the same, it was only if you changed the tune they sounded different.

'But then she got mad and said she would give the story to one of the Boston newspapers. He told her to go ahead...and that's okay, I know there's no proof, but there'd be enquiries, and a scandal, and what that could do to him! I mean, it all being mixed up with the Stonors. She can make a heap of trouble,' she finished uncertainly.

I hadn't the heart to tell her that Cassie had probably already delivered her story to the press, today, in person. 'How long have you known her?' I asked.

'Not too long. I met her at the party Rowena gave when she opened her restaurant.'

Outside, the caterer's van pulled away with a noisy grinding of gears. 'Tell me—did Colin use his car this morning?'

'Why no, we walked up to the golf course. I went with him. I've decided to learn.'

'Sebastian's car was out of action, wasn't

it? Remember, he said he'd pulled a muscle jacking it up.'

'Kind of funny he should wear a plaster on his arm for that.'

'A plaster? You're sure?'

'Sure I'm sure. I saw it when he reached for the sugar. Charlotte, what are you getting at?'

'I'm not sure myself. I need time to work this out.' Telling myself to think logically, take it one step at a time, I couldn't stop the joy that had its bubbling source somewhere inside me. I had just realised that Miranda Martell's ideas of what constituted a distinguished-looking man and mine didn't coincide.

I had looked doubtfully at the only dress I had to wear for the celebrations this evening, wondering if it wasn't too formal, but having seen the preparations below I decided to wear it after all. It was new, below-the-knee length, black and crepey, with bootlace shoulder straps and hip-hugging skirt that flared out towards the hem. When I put it on, I saw at once the colour wasn't going to do much for me tonight. It made too obvious the lilac shadows under my eyes, underlined my natural pallor. Excitement, apprehension, took me like that. It didn't matter. This was Isabella's evening, and I wasn't aiming to outstage her.

We met in the hall and sipped sherry from fine old glass, waiting for the guests to arrive—about a hundred and fifty people: friends, cousins, other well-heeled Bostonians who had their summer homes around here, and for most of whom this was an annual event. When, later, I saw their clothes I was glad I hadn't changed.

'Yon's a verra sexy dress ye're wearin', lassie,' whispered Colin, stage-Scottish, when he saw me. Max didn't say anything, but he looked. And when, for want of somewhere to hide my own feelings, I turned my attention back to Colin, I saw the reason for his uncharacteristic flippancy was relief, pure and simple. He had got himself back on a firm footing, reinstated himself with Harmony, dealt with Cassie. I hoped that by choosing to do so in his blunt and forthright way he hadn't made the situation considerably worse. Cassie Hayter was a dangerous woman. Cassie, and Sebastian...

I looked at Sebastian. Smiling and smiling, that secret, veiled smile. When his eyes rested on me, I felt as cold as though a snake had slithered over me.

The party lurched towards semi-success, a staid affair by today's standards, the men in an amazing array of sportswear, the women glossy as blackbirds in simple Fifth Avenue casual clothes that must have cost a fortune.

There was dancing on the lawn to piped music, but it was so hot only a few people availed themselves of the opportunity, the younger element who were very much in the minority. The rest sat or stood in groups on the terrace or around the tables set up in the garden, under the swags of coloured lights, without too much vulgar enthusiasm, here because it was a prestigious event in the social calendar. Isabella saw that I was introduced to her guests, every one; they welcomed me with genuine warmth, issued hospitable invitations, friendly and anxious that I should take home a good impression of America. None of those old enough to have known my mother mentioned her.

I had just finished dancing, sweatily clasped in the arms of a young cousin who'd have been drunker if he dared, who was telling me he couldn't wait for his vacation in London, man. 'Boy, it really swings here,' he said in disgust, and asked before relinquishing me if he might look me up during his vacation. I said he could, hoping he wasn't expecting too much of London, and then I saw Max.

When my partner had left me, Max came across and took my arm. 'Do you want anything to eat?' he asked, jerking his head to where Roscoe in a tall chef's hat was barbecuing steaks and chicken drumsticks.

I shook my head, and we sat down on the grass. 'Where have you been all evening?'

'Looking for Sebastian.'

I hadn't seen him either, since that half-hour before the guests arrived. 'Why do you want him?'

'It doesn't matter, he'll be found,' he said oddly, then, 'I'm expecting a telephone call, from Bernie Fisher to be precise. When it comes, I have to go and meet him at Cassie Hayter's shop. She's been out all day, but he'll call me as soon as she returns.'

'I think she's gone to Boston.'

'That blackmail business? Apparently you were right, and Cassie was attempting to blackmail Harmony, but it seems Colin's coped very effectively with her.' He was dismissive, partly, I suspected, from a reluctance to discuss the details of the affair—it must have been Colin who had told him, and an uneasy confrontation that must have been—nevertheless, he evidently approved of the line Colin had taken. 'Don't worry. She won't have been to any newspaper, not with what she has to hide. She was trying it on.'

I said, 'Who is Bernie Fisher? Why is he watching her shop? He's a policeman, isn't he? Not a connoisseur of old silver.'

'Oh, he's that too. He's a detective, yes, but he's an expert all right about silver, about old jewellery, too—stealing it, breaking it up, resetting it.'

'Isabella's sapphire and diamond necklace?'

'That's right!' He gave me a pretty sharp glance. 'What has Isabella told you about that?'

'Only that it's missing—and that she thinks Rowena took it.'

He was silent for several moments. 'So that's what she was trying to make herself believe, fooling herself to the last.'

'It's what she told me.'

'Well I reckon she's faced the truth now. You know she and Rowena had a long talk this afternoon? No? Well she's lodged a formal notice of theft with the police against Sebastian. And you know what that means?' His face looked grim in the semi-light under the trees.

'Yes, Max, I think I do.'

'It's a big admission for her to make.'

It was hard for him too. Hard for him to admit that where Lois had been concerned he had been unable to help. I knew this was what he had been trying to say when the window had broken.

'Lois told me Isabella had given her the necklace,' he said. 'I'd no reason to disbelieve it; Isabella stifled her with presents...then when Fisher came along... he'd been investigating Cassie Hayter, and Sebastian too, for some time. They've been suspected of working together, Sebastian receiving the stolen jewellery, Cassie re-working it to sell again. Now it seems her former partner is prepared to give evidence.'

I could feel nothing for Sebastian, or Cassie; I could think only of Rowena, and what she must face.

'Fisher's not too pleased about Isabella's

failure to report the necklace stolen until now,' Max said. 'He wants me there when he confronts Cassie Hayter, to identify the necklace if she still has it, or even part of it. It's possible she has. They've been lying low lately, probably had an idea they were being watched.'

'Yes, Lois's death would have made them careful. Oh, Max—'

'You find it incredible, don't you, that Lois would steal from Isabella of all people? You'd have had to know her to understand. She was simply—unprincipled. I don't believe she had any ideas of right and wrong. She would rationalise anyway that the necklace would come to her when Isabella died, so what the hell? That's what I tell myself, anyway.'

I hated the bitterness in his voice.

The first rain began to fall in great heavy splashes. There was a concerted rush for the house, but the rain didn't amount to much. Within a few seconds it had stopped again.

'Let me come with you when you go down to meet Fisher.'

'Charlotte, I don't want you mixed up in this.' His voice was rough.

'I'll stay in the car. I just want to go with

you.' I could never have imagined what a tremendous relief it would be to admit it, that it was all I ever wanted, simply to be near him, to be with him.

He reached a hand out and gently, so gently, touched my face. And smiled. And said, 'You'd better pick up some more suitable clothes and have them ready in my car, then. The rain's going to come down in earnest any minute.' His voice was almost as unsteady as mine.

I flew upstairs, grabbed some flat shoes and headscarf and rolled them up in my white raincoat. Down the back stairs, meeting nobody. Across to where the Pontiac was garaged in one of the outbuildings, to stuff my bundle under the front passenger seat. I was just in time to get back into the house before the deluge began. The party was over.

During the next hour, the packed house grew more and more steamy as the rain thundered down, accompanied by a right royal thunder storm. Some attempt was made to carry on with the party atmosphere, a little dancing went on, but in reality everyone was merely waiting until the storm cleared enough for them to leave.

As suddenly as it had started, the rain stopped. People began to make their goodbyes and paddle out to their cars. Within half an hour, the last guest had departed.

12

The hall, with its carpets rolled back and its furniture pushed to the walls, looked immense, echoing and slightly intimidating. The candles guttered low, throwing leaping shadows on to the coffered ceiling. The atmosphere was intensely humid, a damp, close heat that was enervating and depressing, despite the high wind that had sprung up, rattling the window frames and tossing the branches of the trees outside, but doing nothing to cool the air.

Isabella went to the corner between the stairs and the huge fireplace and took her usual seat in her high-backed chair, motioning us to the others grouped around the oak table. She leaned back, resting her elbows on the chair arms. 'I'm so tired,' she said at last. 'I can't keep it up any longer. It's time they all knew, Max.'

'No!' he came back strongly.

Faintly, a smile crossed her face. 'Are you afraid?'

'I won't allow you to do this.'

'Won't? Won't, to me? Don't go too far!' Her smile faded, her autocratic spirit kindling at any attempt to resist her. I doubt whether the double-edged remark was lost on anyone there. She wasn't in any way above using her hitherto despised frailty to get what she wanted, though at this moment she appeared anything but a weak old woman with a bad heart. She had clearly not been referring to her physical state when she had said she was tired. Indeed, the events of the evening, perhaps even what had happened during the day, too, seemed to have injected her with an incandescent energy. She burned like a flame as she sat, very upright.

Max gave her a straight look as adamant as her own, then with a tight whiteness round his mouth he shrugged and leaned against the panelling of the staircase as if in final acceptance of what was to come. Behind him, the tapestry on the rising wall of the stairs flickered and moved in the leaping, dying flames of the candles. Terror for him swamped any other feelings, and I edged closer to him, wanting to offer him the comfort of nearness, needing his reassuring touch myself. But he held himself away from me.

The rain again drummed on the terrace, a sad, mournful ending to the evening, but the thunder and lightning had stopped. One of the candles in the nearest sconce spluttered, almost died. Colin made a sudden, impatient gesture and got up, snuffed it out completely and switched on the lamp. Its gentle radiance spread a warm, comforting glow and gathered the group together, the gloom of the rest of the hall receding into sepia shadow.

Isabella was in no hurry, looking calmly at each one of us in turn, assessing, perhaps, our reactions to what she was about to say. Her eyes followed Colin as he came back to perch on the arm of Harmony's chair, moved to Rowena. Then rested on myself, thoughtfully. Then she spoke, without preliminaries, her normally quick strong voice perhaps slower than usual, but still ringing and vibrant. 'Things have gone too far. I see I must tell you the truth of what happened on the night Lois died. Sparing no one,' she added, bending a long look on Max which he met without flinching.

'The night she died, she came to me with a request for money. I refused. I told her it must stop, all of it, this recklessness with money, with men...oh, I wasn't blind! I had tried to shut my eyes to it, yes, but she was creating a scandal, she was smirching the Stonor name, and that I simply would not have. She became very excited and I'm afraid we both said bitter things which would have been better left unsaid. Things which had nothing whatever to do with what we were talking about—and at last she flung out of the room in a temper.'

A spasm of pain, quickly mastered, crossed her face and she was swept back into the incident. 'She was such a beautiful child,' she said inconsequentially, 'so like Lydia. Like sunshine—and flawed, like her.'

I made an instinctive movement, but Max's outflung hand restrained me, warning me not to interrupt, and Isabella went on. 'Never had she spoken to me like that, never said such unforgivable, unforgettable things. I think it was then that I began to face the unpalatable truth, that I was to blame for what she had become. I had been a failure, as far as bringing up my children was concerned.' She was, as she had said, not sparing herself. It was painful to see. 'We are supposed to learn from experience, to become wiser the older we grow. Never believe it, any of you. We go on making the same mistakes over and over, from the cradle to the grave. I spoiled one daughter. I lost her. And I learned nothing, nothing...until it was too late—'

'Grandmother—' Rowena began, taken out of her own preoccupation, scorched with pity.

Isabella warned her to silence. 'I couldn't sleep after that. I wasn't feeling too well, and at last I got up again and dressed and went to look for Lois. I couldn't leave things as they were. There had been a terrible atmosphere in the house for days; she had been upsetting everyone. We had to come to some basis of agreement. She wasn't in her room, but when I went downstairs I saw Max and he told me he'd left her on the beach half an hour ago. I pretended it didn't matter, and let him think I was going back up to bed, because I knew he'd have stopped me from going down to her. But it was an opportunity I didn't want to miss. After a swim in the bay, Lois was always calmer, and I hoped we would be able to talk.'

She looked down at her hands. Her fingers were clasped so tightly together the rings bit into the thin flesh. 'She was there, sure enough. She was walking away from me, the dogs following her, and when she reached the rocks, she stood on the highest one, the one she used to dive from, looking down into the water. When she heard me coming, she turned round. She was furious when she saw me. She said defiantly, "So now you're following me around? Or have you come seeking an apology?" I took hold of her and shook her. I said, "You're not a child, so stop acting like one." And she slipped, backwards, between the rocks. It was over, as quickly as that.'

A current of shock ran through the whole group, like an electric circuit. For the first time, Isabella faltered. The excitement that had sustained her had left her. Her pallor was intense. Colin made a movement towards her, looking at Max, but she held up her hand. 'A few more minutes, please. I pulled her out of the water. She was wedged between two sharp boulders, but I guess fear gave me strength. She was dead when I finally pulled her out and laid her on the beach. As I went back up the path the dogs began to howl.'

Harmony said, 'Grandma, don't—'

Isabella didn't seem to hear her. 'I went for Max and told him what had happened. He insisted on my going straight to my room—I was feeling pretty bad by that time—and then Roscoe came and he went down to the beach with him.'

It was amazing that she had survived the incident, struggling with the dead weight of Lois's body, then clambering back up that difficult, precipitous path. *It amounts to murder.* That's what she had said, according to Colin, but no one could ever have seriously believed that.

'Will you help me to my room, Rowena?'

'I'll come and see you settled,' Max said. 'Will somebody please fetch Mary?'

There was no thought of going to bed, but nothing to say, either. Harmony, after going in search of Mary, came back with a tray of coffee. We sat around drinking it, she and Colin and myself, saying nothing. It seemed like hours later that Max came down again, but it couldn't have been. The coffee pot was still hot, and I poured him a cup.

'She's comfortable, and she wants to see you,' he said to me. 'I've told her you must only stay a minute...I've sedated her, and she'll be feeling drowsy before long.'

I promised and shot upstairs, pulling back my running footsteps to a quiet walk as I approached her bedroom. Mary McDermott opened the door at my soft tap. 'Don't let her tire herself now, will you?'

'I've already promised Max I won't.'

'What are you whispering about? Come here, Charlotte.'

Mary left and I went to the bed where Isabella was propped on pillows, wearing an uncompromising white nightdress, her silver-threaded black hair braided. Her hands on the coverlet looked strangely bare without their quota of heavy rings. She was not unchanged by what had happened during the last hours—she had the drawn look of someone after a long illness—but she had lost none of her presence, that authority she would keep to the end.

'Sit down,' she commanded. 'I want to talk to you.'

'Now Grandmother, Max has told me you must be quiet. I'm only to be allowed to stay for a minute.'

She stared at me, then her strong severe face crumpled into that unnervingly sweet smile that was always so unexpected. 'That's the first time you've ever called me that.'

'What?'

'Grandmother. Ever since you came here you've managed very well not to address me at all by name.'

Shamed, I tried to conceal my distress, knowing it was probably true, though subconscious. She had never felt like my grandmother before and yet now, despite all that had happened, perhaps because of it, my feelings towards her were warmer than ever before.

'It won't take longer than a minute to say what I have to.' She stretched out a hand for mine, held it between her palms, and this physical contact, too, was something new between us. 'I haven't got long, Charlotte, my life's finished—no, not maybe today, maybe next year...but not long.'

I found my eyes blurred with tears, and I was startled when she asked, softly, 'Why didn't you persist in asking me about your mother?'

Isabella had never had any time for prevarication, her own or anyone else's. 'I asked you once and you refused. You wouldn't have told me, however many times I asked.'

The smallest quiver of a smile crossed her face. 'Forthright Charlotte! You're quite right, neither would I, I guess. I vowed that old scandal would never be continued into this generation.' She closed her eyes for a moment, and when she opened them, she said, 'It seems—it seems I am defeated. Rowena tells me she already knows, and that you have found Ralph's diaries.' She gave a small, painful sigh and sank further back into the mound of pillows. 'I want you to know everything. The rest of those pages are in this envelope. Take it. It isn't the whole story, but Mary McDermott will finish it.'

I took the large, well-filled manilla envelope that lay on the bedside table and held it. 'You knew about the diaries all the time. You tore those pages out.'

She moved her head from side to side. 'Life can still hold surprises. You can live with a man half a lifetime and still not know everything about him. I knew nothing of this novel—or the diary—until the quarrel with Lois—the night she died. She let slip something about your mother which I was certain no one else but me, and perhaps Mary, knew. I asked her how she knew, and when she told me about the diaries I made her give those pages to me...'

Her grip on my hand was loosening, her face had gone slack. She was almost asleep, her eyes closing and her voice faint as temple wind-bells. 'Try not to think too badly of me when you read the truth...I loved her so much.'

The envelope in my hands, I bent down and kissed her dry, papery cheek. 'Goodnight, Grandmother. Sleep well.'

Mary came in and as I left the room was lowering her pillow, tucking in the coverlet.

The telephone was ringing as I came out of her room, and I stood waiting at the foot of the stairs. Within minutes, Max had joined me. There was something I didn't like about his expression. 'Go and wait for me in the car,' he said in a low voice. 'I need my bag.'

'What's happened?'

'There's been a fire. Cassie's shop has been on fire.'

Shock gave impetus to my feet. I raced outside and towards the outbuildings. By the time Max joined me I had slipped out of my high heels and into my flat shoes, belted on my raincoat and was waiting in the passenger seat. He threw his doctor's bag into the back, switched on, did a swift reverse out and we were off down the drive. Halfway down, he braked to a sudden halt. Across the drive was a tree, a half-dead beech, the branches waving dementedly in the wind. Swearing softly, he threw the Pontiac into reverse again. 'Is there another way?' I asked.

'Yup, by sea! Still want to come?'

The white speedboat with *Dolphin* lettered in gold on its side bobbed in the shallows, the engine ticking over. From the front seat, through the windscreen, the sea looked wild and black. Only choppy, Max grinned, but I held my breath, praying I wouldn't be seasick.

'Ready?' he asked, and I nodded, huddled beside him in the oilskins he had tossed to me. 'Then hold tight!'

The engine roared and we shot straight forward at hair-raising speed, cutting through the water so that it curved away in inky glass wings on either side of us. I felt Max touch my arm, and turned to face him. 'Okay?' he shouted. I couldn't hear the words, only see his lips moving, so I nodded my head vigorously for reply, and he grinned and stuck his thumb up. His hands gripping the wheel, he looked taut with purpose, as if he felt this was the way everything should be tackled, head on, full throttle.

Suddenly, I found that I too was enjoying the exhilarating sensation of tremendous speed. There were white caps on the waves all around us, the sky was dense and black above. Once or twice a flash of blue-white lightning rent the clouds apart, thunder rumbled distantly, and the windscreen was beaded with spray as the boat kept to its arrow-straight course. Then he was swinging the boat round so that we caught the current and that wasn't so pleasant, making my stomach lurch disagreeably. A minute or two later we were into calmer waters and running in slowly beside the pier. Max cut the motor and made fast at the foot of the wooden steps.

When we climbed to the top Bernie Fisher, who had seen our arrival, was waiting for us, and accompanied us towards what had once been the pretty little boutique.

It hadn't been much as fires go, but then it hadn't needed much to destroy such a small building. Smoke had been seen coming from the back of the premises Fisher told us. The fire brigade had been sent for, but even before it arrived the rain had started, too late to save Cassie's shop, but soon enough to prevent it spreading to the places either side. There was nothing left now but the shell.

A small knot of spectators was being dispersed by the police, and four of them were manhandling Cassie's big safe into a van. At that moment a burly sergeant emerged from the gaping doorway. 'Over here, Bernie! Tell the young lady to keep back there please, but if that's the doc you have there with you better bring him. We've found the girl.'

I stood waiting on the pier, shivering with dread and cold, my hands stuck deep into my pockets. The rain began again in a mournful drizzle, intensifying the bitter, acrid odour emanating from the burned building. I pulled my headscarf from my pocket and tied it on. When I'd finished Mrs Martell from the gallery next door was beside me, her hand on my arm, asking me if I'd like to wait inside. I wanted to decline; it didn't seem to me to be a moment for gossip or speculation. Then I saw how nervously she puffed at her cigarette, that the fingers holding it were trembling. The last hour or so hadn't been too good for Miranda Martell, either.

I thanked her and followed her into her shop, perching on a stool by the counter. She went into the back and presently returned with two steaming mugs of coffee, one of which she thrust into my hands. I sipped gratefully. She had put brandy or something into it, which soon warmed my hands and feet, but failed to get through to the icy core inside me.

'I heard them say they'd found her. I sure had some lucky escape there,' she said at last when she saw my teeth had stopped chattering, and her pale, frantic glance skittered round the wild splashes of colour bought by the tourists to remind them of their holidays, through which she made her livelihood. 'That poor, poor girl,' she added. 'What had she done to deserve that?'

She saw my look, and stopped, then went on rapidly, unable to help herself, 'I'll tell you something. That yellow Chevy was here again, just before I smelled that smoke.'

The door opened and it was Max, looking for me. Mrs Martell, when he inquired, showed him where he might wash his hands, and by the time he came back she was repeating what she'd told me to Fisher, who had followed him in.

'You're sure of that, Mrs Martell?' Fisher asked. 'You'd be prepared to testify?'

'I'm sure. He parked out back and I saw him when I was getting my dinner. It was that light-haired guy came here this morning, so I reckoned Cassie was back. I just finished my steak and then I went to tell her about the English girl—about you,' she nodded in my direction, in case there should be some mistake, 'and that was how I saw the smoke. If I'd gone right away, maybe I'd have been in time...' she ended unhappily.

'No, Mrs Martell, I guess you wouldn't,' Fisher said. 'According to Dr Remmick here she's been dead for some time, maybe since this morning.'

'Oh my gosh! She's been in there, dead, all the *time?*' Then, rounding on him, 'How come you didn't prevent it? You've been hanging around here long enough.'

'Mrs Martell, we weren't keeping a constant surveillance on her. Only waiting to question her in connection with a certain matter.'

It had to be asked. 'How did she die?'

It was Max who answered me. 'She'd apparently been hit on the temple by a sort of rock with some pink crystals in it.'

'A geode.'

'Yes, I believe that is what they are known as, Miss Haigh.'

'Do you mean she was murdered?' I swallowed, trying hard to concentrate on anything other than the fact that I had probably held that lovely, heavy rock in my hands a couple of days before. 'That whoever did it came back and set fire to the shop to cover up?'

'I'm not saying anything, not until Forensic has been here.'

We said goodbye to Mrs Martell, I thanked her for the coffee, she said I was welcome, and as we went outside Fisher added, 'Or at any rate, not until we've picked up Sebastian Garth.'

The rain was now nearly as heavy as during the thunderstorm, and Lieutenant

Fisher, who was to come back with us to Stonor's Point, suggested that we leave the speedboat to be collected later and drive back with him.

13

The storm of the previous night had dissipated the heat, and the morning was sharp and clear, cool enough for sweater and jeans. No one else was stirring as I let myself out into the garden, past the party wreckage, the doused barbecue and the drowned tables.

I had the curious light emptiness within me that comes from being without sleep, going with an intense awareness of all around me. Everything sparkled, the sun, the wet grass which drenched my feet as I crossed it to go through the woods, drawn to the solitude of the beach and the sea. I walked with buoyant steps, as if a cushion of air was between me and the ground. And I was heavy as lead inside.

Reaching the beach, I walked to the first of the flat rocks and sat down, staring out to sea, my hands balled into fists within my pockets. I knew the full story now. I had opened Pandora's box and nothing was going to put back the lid on what I had released.

It seemed funny now—no, no, my God, anything but funny. Ironic maybe, pathetic certainly—to think how eagerly I'd begun on those last pages Grandmother had given me. They had been quickly read. How long it would take me to accept them was another matter.

The facts which concerned me began shortly after Ellen had come back home to live, just after George Allot had been posted to Korea. Lydia by then was at Vassar, and gratified reports of her progress were duly entered in the diary. It had been a time of unalloyed happiness for Ralph, the long summer spent here at Stonor's Point with his beloved elder daughter and the child, Rowena, to enchant his days.

Then the bubble burst. Lydia came home, announcing, to their stunned disbelief, that she had left college because she had become pregnant, but refusing to name the father. The summer before my birthday the following year.

I had known, ever since seeing Lydia's marriage certificate, that I had been conceived out of wedlock. It had surprised me, but it hadn't mattered. I could see, however, that it would have mattered to people of my mother's generation, with their different attitudes. And especially to this old starchy New England family. But, reading the diaries, I couldn't understand why my mother wouldn't acknowledge John Haigh, or marry him. Clearly, her family would not have approved her choice, unendowed as my father was with this world's goods, but, knowing him, they could not have failed to respect and like him. As it was, my mother brought on to herself the backlash of Isabella's humiliation, her father's disappointment, the shame and disgrace both of them felt. Lydia, fortune's darling, their golden girl, a blossom in the dust! It seemed the days passed in wrangles, in endless plans by Isabella to hush up what was clearly to be regarded as a deadly secret. At least they hadn't actually thrown her out.

Then the pressure on her had been unexpectedly relieved, though in a way even she could not have wished for. The news of George Allot's death in action eclipsed for a time even Lydia's disgrace. Poor Ellen was utterly distraught. No one, not her father, nor even the five year old Rowena, could comfort her. She was inconsolable. 'Sometimes I fear for her sanity,' wrote her father. 'It is scarcely natural, grief like this.'

An Army officer called, with the unenviable task of bringing George's personal belongings which had been flown home from Korea. For two days afterwards Ellen stayed in her room, refusing to come out. On the third morning, she was found dead of an overdose of sleeping pills.

Why, Ralph demanded of himself, torn in two by grief, why? Until, clearing up Ellen's things, he had found the letter amongst George's returned effects, and had known why.

At one in the morning, I had been sitting with the papers still in front of me when Mary McDermott knocked on my bedroom door and came in bearing coffee and biscuits on a tray. When she had closed the door, she poured out two cups. 'So you've finished reading now, Charlotte?' she asked as she brought mine to me, and for a moment her kindly, sympathetic hand rested lightly on my shoulder.

I nodded. 'How long have you known?'

'About your father? Only since your grandmother gave me those papers to read.

I already knew the rest. Oh, we weren't supposed to know that Lydia was pregnant, but you can't keep a thing like that secret. What a time that was, three tragedies, one on top of the other like that.'

'*Three?* Oh yes, I suppose to my grandparents, my mother being pregnant would be a tragedy. Especially—' I broke off, unable to go on.

'No, I meant your granda's death.'

It was suddenly necessary to hold my coffee cup in both hands in order to put it down safely. 'How—did he die?'

'Oh, pneumonia, but...well, you know by what he wrote how he felt when he read that letter amongst Captain Allot's papers. He sent me to fetch Lydia to the study, and I knew something dreadful was happening in the family. I'd never heard him in such a rage. He was usually mild-tempered, a lovely man, but that day you could hear him all over the house. I thought he would surely kill her, and I was just plucking up courage to go in and stop it when your mother came out of the study, all white-faced, and rushed upstairs, right past her mother. Your grandma, she just stood there at the top of the steps, listening, and God help me I never again want to see a look like there was on her face when Lydia pushed past her!'

'So she knew, as well, she's always known.'

Mary nodded. 'I reckon your granda showed her that letter before he faced Lydia with it. Well, he came out of the study after her and went out, just as he was, without so much as a jacket to cover himself, and it raining cats and dogs. Nobody dared try to stop him and he came back hours later, soaked to the skin. He caught a terrible chill that turned to pneumonia. He wasn't ever a strong man, your granda, and he died a couple of days later, God rest him.'

I pressed my hands to my temples, oppressed beyond belief by these old horrors.

'Oh, the atmosphere in this house!' Mary declared, pouring on another thick layer of drama. 'The two of them, Lydia and Mrs Stonor, like two black ghosts, hardly speaking to each other before the funeral. Mrs Stonor, she said to me, "She's no longer my daughter, Mary," as if Lydia were to blame for everything that had happened. Lydia wouldn't so much as open her mouth. She stayed until the funeral and then she left, and she never came back.'

I stared out across the sea that went straight across to England—if it wasn't for Ireland in between, I thought with a half-hysterical laugh—and tried to fight down the anger against my mother.

'There's no such thing as love at first sight,' I confidently told my father, once.

'Oh yes, there is. It took me ten minutes, maybe less, to fall in love with your mother.'

So that was how it had been with him. And he had married her, knowing she was carrying another man's child. He must have known—by then it would have been obvious—and in any case I knew my mother would never have practised that particular deception. What I would never know was how she had felt, whether her love for him had grown out of gratitude, or whether my father...

He wasn't my father. I was not, and never had been, John Haigh's loved and wanted child.

It was George Allot whom Lydia had been meeting in secret while she was at college and he was stationed nearby.

When she had written George that fatal letter after he had been sent to Korea, telling him she was pregnant, she had also told him all was over between them, that she hadn't known what madness had overtaken her. She didn't know what she was going to do—it would depend on how her parents took the news—but she swore that she would never reveal him as the father of her child.

The pebble I was clutching bit into my hand. I threw it out towards the sea. Her own sister! Poor Ellen, unloved Ellen, whose only hope she had stolen, she who could have had any man she wanted, gay, shallow, thoughtless, *loved* Lydia.

But she had been none of these things when I loved her, she had undergone a personality change so radical she was simply not the same person. If George Allot hadn't been killed, if that letter from Lydia hadn't been so cruelly returned to Ellen, there would have been a very different story. As it was, my mother must have lived all these years with feelings of remorse and guilt for the death of her sister and her father. I thought she had paid her debt.

Footsteps scrunched along the shingle. I

came back from a very long way away, and waited until Max reached me. He put both hands down to pull me to my feet, and held me hard against the strong, powerful beat of his heart.

My grandmother died three weeks later, in her sleep, here at Stonor's Point, not at the Beacon Hill house as she had predicted.

The evening before I left for England, Max and I took our favourite walk down through the woods and along the seashore. 'Just you make sure you get back here as quick as you can,' he said. 'Don't forget you have one or two pressing things to attend to. Like a small matter of getting married.'

'That? I can easily push that in between writing my historical novel and the history of the Stonor Family.'

He laughed, drew my arm through his and tucked it against his side. 'She'd have been glad to hear you say that, about the family history.'

'She knew, Max. I told her before she died.'

During those three weeks Isabella and I had come to know and to respect each other. Love was too strong a word, I thought, though maybe not. Love itself was an infinitely variable emotion, as I was beginning to discover. From the deep and tender, passionate and strong feelings between myself and the man who walked beside me, to the tentative developing relationship with my half-sister Rowena, which would in time, I hoped, come under the heading of love. I already knew that beneath her brittle nervous exterior she had a warm and loving heart. She had showed this in her feelings for my grandmother and in the natural delicacy that had wanted to prevent me knowing the truth about my father.

'John Haigh was my true father,' I had been able to say at last, realising the reality, repeating what Harmony, wiser than I in this sense, had said of Richard Stonor. My father, not through an accident of birth, but through years of love and wisdom and caring. But I said it to Max, not Rowena. Some things are better left unsaid.

I would never know, for instance, how much Rowena had known about Sebastian's activities, or how far he had gone in his attempts to prevent Isabella leaving me her fortune, because I would never ask her. Fisher's theory was that

Sebastian had not known that Cassie, desperately short of money this last year, had been blackmailing Harmony until he had overheard me telling Max on the terrace, and that this had been the cause of their quarrel. The necklace had not been found. Cassie's safe was quite empty, but the police were confident that when Sebastian was picked up the fingerprints over the safe and elsewhere in the shop would be found to be his. I wasn't so sure they ever would pick him up. An eel was easy to hold in comparison with Sebastian Garth.

When Isabella's will was read, it was found to be the one she had made almost a year before which, according to Edward Bruce, she had not spoken of changing. She had left everything to be divided between her four granddaughters, or their heirs. In this context, she included Harmony and my daughter Lydia's daughter, Charlotte Haigh, at present living in England. This meant that Max would receive Lois's share; together with my portion, this would go a long way to realising his dream of a private clinic. And tonight I had some marvellous news which I had waited until now to impart: Rowena and Harmony had also decided to put their share of the inheritance into the clinic. Rowena said she was content with what her business provided. Harmony felt that she had more than enough with what Richard had left her. She would find something to do with that after she had graduated and she and Colin had gone to live in Scotland.

Max and I were to live here, where he could continue his career and I would devote myself wholeheartedly to fulfilling my ambition for historical writing.

We turned back, leaving wet footprints at the water's edge. Above us on the cliffs, the house stood black against the evening sky. A light was switched on at one of the windows.

Behind us the tide, coming in, covered the bleached bones of the wrecked boat and rose above the big grey rocks.

The publishers hope that this book has given you enjoyable reading. Large Print Books are especially designed to be as easy to see and hold as possible. If you wish a complete list of our books, please ask at your local library or write directly to: Magna Large Print Books, Long Preston, North Yorkshire, BD23 4ND, England.